MIXING UP MURDER

Little Dog Diner, Book 1

EMMIE LYN

Sweet Promise press
PO Box 72
Brighton, MI 48116

For Melissa.
Thank you for believing in me.

ABOUT THIS BOOK

Murder wasn't supposed to be on the menu at the Little Dog Diner, but that's exactly what we got served anyway.

Hi, I'm Dani Mackenzie and I'm the unfortunate soul who owns said diner. Looks like business is going to be slow for a little while as the whole town scrambles to find whodunnit.

At first I just needed something to keep me busy while on my forced vacation, but now as the clues stack up, I'm caught in the middle of this crazy mixed-up murder. And I'll do anything to get to the bottom of what really happened and why it happened in my kitchen.

Too bad the only known witness to the crime is the victim's terrier, Pip, and no one believes she bludgeoned her owner to death. But if not her… then who? And, perhaps more importantly, who's next?

AUTHOR'S NOTE

Hi cozy readers!

Welcome to Misty Harbor on Blueberry Bay on the coast of Maine where cozy mysteries abound. You are about to meet Dani Mackenzie, her grandmother Rose, and her spirited Jack Russell Terrier, Pip, along with many other great characters. Sit back and enjoy!

Click here to sign up for my newsletter and never miss a new release.

CHAPTER ONE

"Why did I ever let you talk me into going to Ray's funeral?"

I didn't really expect my best friend, Lily, to answer me. She just gave me one of her looks. The one that talked me into spending a beautiful Monday morning attending a service at Two Wilde Funeral Home for someone I never even liked.

As though I had nothing better to do.

But… what do you do when your best friend needs you at an unpleasant affair? You put on your best little black dress, hold her hand and your nose, and hope for the best.

"Dani," Lily said, tenderly tucking one of my wayward curls behind my ear. My attempt to control my mass of auburn hair with a tiny silver hair clip failed miserably. Several curlicues always refused to cooperate. "Thanks for coming with me," she said in her musical voice. She completely ignored my discomfort and slipped her arm in mine. "I can't believe Ray died before the divorce became final." Then she maneuvered me toward the funeral home.

We took the steps up to the columned entrance of Two Wilde two at a time, late as usual because Lily got hung up worrying how she looked. She thought black made her long, blonde hair fade to a washed-out cream. I had to talk her out of an electric blue, figure-hugging sheath. "Sure, it makes your hair look like a crown of spun gold," I told her. "But you'll never live down the snide *merry widow* jokes in this town.

As far as her comment about her husband's death was concerned, I should say I was shocked, but I couldn't, because I wasn't.

Lily's soon to be ex-husband had been a worthless piece of scum as a husband, but on paper, he owned a lot of real estate in Misty Harbor, Maine, the picturesque town where we lived. Now everything would go to Lily. I couldn't be happier for her. And, I admit, I was a teensy bit jealous. She was set for life. And me? I'd be working my fingers off feeding the locals at the Little Dog Diner for, well, forever.

Don't get me wrong. I loved our diner. Yes, *our* —my grandma, Rose Mackenzie who owned the building and took care of the books, and Lily and I who did the day to day cooking and serving—had our own business, the Little Dog Diner. So, Lily wasn't just my best friend, but my business partner as well. I had an interest in her future, but who could blame her for choosing financial freedom over working? Um, no one.

I pulled the heavy wood door of Two Wilde Funeral Home open, pasted an appropriately somber expression on my face, smoothed any wrinkles out of my black dress, and followed my friend inside.

The door clicked shut behind us and all heads turned in our direction. A few gasps and whispers by Ray's family along the lines of, "I can't believe Lily brought Danielle Mackenzie," followed those head turns, but we stared straight ahead, locked our arms, and made our way to the casket.

An open casket.

Surrounded by white lilies.

"You didn't warn me about that," I hissed in

Lily's ear as I jabbed her in the side, harder than I intended.

She winced. "Would you have come?" she whispered back.

"Of course not." We were three steps away from looking at the dead face of Raymond Lemay, and I didn't know if I'd make it without losing my blueberry muffin. Lily dragged me by the arm, reluctant as I was, up the aisle to the casket. I closed my eyes and let her blindly pull me to the spot I didn't want to be near under any circumstance. The sweet scent from the lilies around the casket was so strong I wanted to fan my hand in front of my face or rush outside to suck in fresh air. I didn't do either.

"This is the best he's ever looked," Lily whispered. "You won't believe it, Dani. His face is actually handsome now that he's relaxed. Open your eyes."

Against my better judgment, I cracked open one eye maybe an eighth of an inch. Then I closed it quickly, took a breath and opened it a sliver again. And held it open. "Okay, not as gruesome as I expected," I admitted.

I opened both eyes and blinked. "Who knew a

dead guy could look this good," I said when I was sure my breakfast would stay put. "He looks like he's sleeping peacefully." Then something caught my eye. Like almost blinding me. "What's that sparkling on his chest?" I whispered to Lily, after checking to be sure no one was watching, I reached in and snatched the item off Ray's shirt. I caught a quick look at what I held in my hand, and saw it was just an earring probably from some weepy relative leaning too far over the body. I tucked it in my pocket to deal with later.

Together, we stared at the pale face, dark hair, and square jaw of Lily's dead husband. Just as we were about to turn around and join the rest of his family, his eyes popped open and he winked.

A blood-curdling shriek filled the hushed room, and then I added my scream to the racket.

Raymond's little terrier, Pip, who had been sitting quietly at one end of the casket with a pink bow clipped on her head, yipped and yapped and charged at us, probably thinking she needed to ward off some terrible spirit about to invade her precious Raymond.

My arms flew up in the air. My silver hair clip popped open, releasing a cascade of crazy curls around my face.

Pip nipped at my ankles.

Lily crashed on to the thick, cushy carpet.

The room fell silent as I tried to make sense of what had happened.

All I could imagine was that Lily had just died from shock right in front of my eyes. Either that, or I had lost my mind. Or both, since the reality was too crazy to believe.

I crouched next to Lily and fanned her pale face with the program I'd grabbed on the way in. "Lily, don't you dare leave me" I ordered. "Come on, open those beautiful blue eyes. You're my best friend in all the world, and I need you to keep me sane, especially in this roomful of your in-laws."

I heard a snort above me. It was a familiar sound. One I'd heard more times than I could remember. The snort that belonged to Lily's almost ex-husband, Raymond, the dead guy who winked at us. A shiver of alarm zinged up my spine.

What was going on?

Lily moaned. I nearly fainted with relief and moved so she'd only be able to see *me* when her eyes opened. "What happened?" she mumbled.

My plan to shield Lily failed. I felt Ray's hot breath on my neck as he crouched next to me. Lily's eyes opened so wide I was afraid they might freeze into a fright mask and never close.

Pip wiggled close to Lily and licked her cheek.

"See, Lily?" Ray said, his voice actually tender. "Pip's thrilled to see you, too."

Lily pushed herself to a sitting position, her cheeks regaining a bit of healthy pink glow. She pointed her finger at Ray. I truly expected to see daggers fly from that finger straight to Ray's heart, sending him back into that white casket he'd recently inhabited. "What the heck is going on?"

"Lily," Ray said in his fake soothing tone as he reached for her hand.

She slapped him.

"You wouldn't answer any of my calls." His whiny voice told me something was up. This guy never begged for anything. He took what he wanted. "I was desperate to talk to you and stop this silly divorce you seem to be intent on carrying out."

"Silly? You think you can sweet talk me after what you did?" Lily pushed herself straighter as her spine seemed to grow a steel rod.

"I said I'm sorry." He even bowed his head a little.

I gagged. My blueberry muffin threatened to make a grand entrance. Again.

My head swiveled between Lily and Ray so fast I thought it might fall off. "Sorry?" I couldn't help but get involved. "If you hadn't put your, you know what, in you know where, we wouldn't be here."

The entire room fell silent. Even Pip sat down. My hand flew to cover my big mouth. "Did I say that out loud?" I asked Lily.

She nodded.

I stood up. "Sorry folks. The shows over." I grabbed Lily's hand and pulled her up next to me. "Let's go. I'll treat you to my latest creation—my blueberry cordial. I think we could both use a shot."

With that, Lily and I, with our heads high, walked past Ray, past his family, past the whispers of, "Did you hear what she said?" We continued to march out the door and down the steps of the white-columned funeral home like the aggrieved widow Lily should have been, leaning on her bestie for support.

"Too bad all that money will stay in his bank account now," I said, steering Lily to the parking lot. I did my best to console her with my arm around her waist as we continued to my car.

And I meant it. I really wanted the best for my friend, even though I had very recently experienced a small pang of envy.

"Oh, Dani," she said with a shrug. "It's never been about the money for me. When I first met

Ray, he was the sweetest, kindest guy I'd ever dated. It was love at first sight. But…"

I bit my tongue since I'd never seen that sweet, kind side of Ray Lemay. He'd always had an ego the size of the ocean and a lust for money that seemed to rule his every action. But who was I to point any of that out to Lily? She'd finally discovered his betrayal when she found him in bed with her cousin. Of course, Ray shed some tears—fake I assumed—and promised Lily the moon, the stars, and a trip to Bali.

Lily had enough sense to walk out on him and serve him with divorce papers. After a little encouragement from *moi* of course, because sometimes your best friend needs more than a helping hand and silent support.

"But what?" I asked, hoping Lily would finish her thought.

"I never told you this because, well, you and Ray never seemed to hit it off."

"I won't argue with that." With my car idling, I asked, "Tell me what, Lil?"

"Ray kept a box full of cards and letters from all of his old flames. I told myself he was being sentimental, but now?" She tilted her head as if trying to solve a puzzle. "Now, I'm not sure what to think."

I decided staying silent, which was hard for me, was possibly the best course of action at the moment. I reached across the seat and squeezed her hand before I pulled away from the funeral home and headed to the Little Dog Diner.

I could feel her eyes on me as she said, "Thanks, Dani. I know I can always count on you. At least we have the diner—you, me, and Rose."

"Yes, I said," keeping my eyes on the traffic but feeling a warm flush at her reminder of our bond."

Until she added, "Ray always hated our arrangement."

"What?" I said, giving her a side eye? "Why? What business was it of his what our arrangement was? Er, is?" A little twang of nervousness clutched at my midsection. Was she about to share another tidbit I wasn't expecting?

I couldn't see the expression on her face when she said, "He thought I should own the building." But I could tell she had turned to me, her seatbelt stretching over the "appropriate" black widow's outfit I'd talked her into wearing. "Do you think Rose would sell it to me?"

"Sell you the diner?" The idea rendered me speechless, well almost. I'd sped the few miles across town, and now I pulled into the narrow strip between two properties owned by my grandmother, Rose Mackenzie: the Little Dog Diner and the historic brick building next door. She had connections in the Blueberry Bay Area, going back generations.

"Actually," Lily said, her voice trembling a bit. "Ray thinks I should own both properties."

My eyebrows hit my hairline. Of course, he does, that slimy real estate investor. "And why does Ray think that's what you should do, Lily? You do realize that Rose has her business in that historic building next to the diner. Do you know how old it is? What would she do with the Blueberry Bay Grapevine? And what about me? Would I have to move out of the apartment above the newspaper?"

This conversation was irritating me to no end. I turned to her and narrowed my eyes. "And why, all of a sudden, are you doing what Ray thinks is best for you?" I smelled something rotten in the air and I didn't like it.

Lily seemed to slink down in her seat. "I didn't think about all that." Was that an apology I heard in her meek voice? I'd take it. After all, she was my best friend.

"This is what I think, Lily." I slid out of my twenty-year-old Honda held together with duct tape. "Ray owns the building on the *other* side of the diner and my guess is he wants to gobble up all the prime real estate on this street for himself. If you're actually still talking to him, tell him he's crazy. Rose will never sell."

We entered the Little Dog Diner through the kitchen. "You first," I said to Lily as I opened the door. I didn't want her to see the expression on my face until I had a chance to get rid of the shock over her absurd suggestion. Sometimes, Lily and I were not on the same page, usually when Ray got himself involved in her life. Too bad the guy was still vertical.

With the diner closed on Monday's, I grabbed a bottle of my blueberry cordial and dragged Lily back outside and up the stairs to my apartment.

A double shot of cordial would help immensely, even if it was only ten in the morning. It was late enough for a drink somewhere, right? Besides, I suspected Lily was holding back a few more tidbits of information about Ray, and I needed to loosen her tongue.

CHAPTER TWO

L ily sank into my overstuffed and threadbare couch with a heavy sigh and a look of defeat. She toed off her sandals and wiggled her feet. "I can't believe Ray faked his own death. How'd he get away with it, anyway?"

From the sad droop of her mouth, I could tell the events of the morning had taken a toll on Lily. "You do know that he owns the Two Wilde Funeral Home building, right? Nick and Frank Wilde probably owed him a favor."

Sometimes I couldn't understand how clueless Lily was. After all, she'd been married to Ray for four years. Didn't she know anything about his real estate business ventures? I sure as heck would have had my nose in all the paperwork.

She sank back into the cushions with a look of dejection that I figured came with the territory if you're going to be involved with someone like Ray. "Yeah, I know that," she said. "But still. It just seems like such a creepy thing to do. You know, lie in a casket? What if someone accidentally closed the lid?" She shuddered. "And what about his family? Everyone was in on it?"

"It sure looks that way, Lil. You know his mother." I tipped my head back so my nose stuck up in the air. "Appearances are everything to her. Plus, she probably couldn't stand the idea that you had the nerve to file for divorce. In her world, it would only work if it had been Ray's idea."

I strutted around the room with my nose up in the air imitating her mother-in-law, both of us laughing until I bumped into the couch and crashed onto Lily. I rolled to my knees and finally managed to get up and pour our drinks. We clinked our glasses together and drained the sweet, blue liquid.

"More?" I asked holding the bottle up ready to refill Lil's glass. "I know *I'm* having seconds."

And then Lil's phone pinged with a text message. She held her glass out and balanced her phone on her lap as she checked the screen. "It's Ray texting me." Her eyebrows crunched together in a puzzled expression. "What do you think he wants?"

I sat on my second-hand coffee table covered with gouges and scratches and filled both glasses. "Well, read it. Maybe he's planning another funeral for himself, but he's giving you a heads up this time." I couldn't resist reminding her of his appalling behavior.

Lily read the message from Ray out loud. "I need to talk to you. Meet me at the diner?"

I sipped my drink. "What are you going to do, Lil? Why do you think Ray wants to meet with you?"

Lily didn't meet my eyes. I'd known her for too long to miss this sure sign that she was hiding something. I leaned closer and rubbed her arm. "What's going on, Lil?"

Tears glistened in Lily's eyes. "I told him it would never work. I told him I couldn't fool *you*, of all people." She finally met my gaze.

"Fool me about what?" A buzz started in my ears. Then a hurtling blow to my gut made me realize that Lily, my best friend in all the world, had gotten involved in some fishy scheme with Ray. I'd sooner trust a rattlesnake with a rat than that man. But…the voice in my head reminded me. No buts. I stood up, forgetting about the glass of blueberry cordial resting on the table next to my leg. Thick, sticky liquid spread in a puddle at my feet. It was just that kind of morning.

"The funeral…" Lily's voice squeaked.

Something in her tone tipped me off. "You knew?" I said, incredulous. My voice raised at least an octave.

"Oh, Dani." Lily followed me to my window where I stood looking at nothing but a bit of Blueberry Bay that glistened beyond the roof-lined street opposite the diner. The beautiful Atlantic Ocean that calmed my spirit and kept me grounded wasn't performing its usual magic at the moment.

I whipped around, sending my curls into a chaotic mess around my face. "His death? Well, that went over like a…a rotten fish stuck in a tailpipe."

"No, not that part. The part about me showing up and embracing him when he really wasn't dead. His family said I'd never come. He wanted to show them I did still love him, and I was calling off the divorce. I know it sounds crazy, but you know Ray —everything had to be over the top."

"Lil, hon, there was no embrace. Or, did I miss that part?"

"You didn't miss what was supposed to be our

emotional reconnection." She hung her head. "I don't know what I was thinking. We talked about a reconciliation, and, at the time, it sounded like a good idea. But when I saw him in the casket, I had second thoughts."

I waited silently.

"I wasn't prepared for him to look so peaceful, so handsome. I guess, to get prepared for the funeral part, I let myself think he *was* dead so, when he winked, I forgot the original plan and fainted. It was all so confusing."

Looking at Lily, so distraught, I had to wrap my arms around her. I really wanted to laugh at the absurdity of this ridiculous plan.

"No worries, Lil. We'll figure something out. But, tell me…why are you two talking about a reconciliation? Wasn't it you who said Ray could rot under a pile of seaweed while the gulls feasted on him?"

"That's before he apologized and promised his fling meant nothing."

Right, I said to myself. Apparently, some people never learn.

"And, he promised to set up an account in my name with one hundred thousand dollars in it."

"He bought you off to stay with him?" I was

flabbergasted that Lily, my dear, sweet, trusting friend could agree to anything so shameless. On the other hand, maybe her plan was to get the money and then divorce him anyway? Now, that would be a smart plan. Or, get the money to buy out the building from Rose. That would be very under-handed indeed.

"Okay, here's what you'll do, Lil." I guided her back to my couch, refilled our glasses of blueberry cordial and reminded myself to make another batch when the next delivery of blueberries arrived.

"Text Ray back and tell him you'll meet him downstairs in the diner in…let's make him sweat a bit. Tell him in an hour. And tell him that account needs to be all set up with the money he promised *before* you meet with him. Okay?"

Lily nodded. I could tell that, at this point, she wasn't going to try to pull anything over on me. She knew I had her back when times were tough, and she also knew I'd never, ever in a gazillion years let Raymond Lemay hurt her again emotionally or otherwise. I think Ray knew it, too.

"I've got one more question before I heat up a bacon, egg, and cheese corn muffin for you." Lily sipped her cordial, a big *what is it* question mark on her face.

"Why drag me into this farce of a funeral?" I asked. "I don't see the point. You could have gone by yourself, had your little make up session and told me about it later."

Lily put her glass down and nodded her agreement before the *but* came. "Ray thought it was better if you came with me. That way, you'd be able to see with your own eyes just how thrilled I was that he wasn't dead—thrilled beyond words, beyond imagination—and that I couldn't live without him. Then you wouldn't argue me out of reconciling with him. That's the way it was *supposed* to go."

Lily's blind spot when it came to Ray Lemay was bigger than the Atlantic Ocean. But I bit my tongue and just nodded as if on some level I understood their ridiculous plan.

"You aren't mad at me, Dani?"

How could I be mad at those big, round, blue eyes staring at me? "I'm not mad, Lil. I can't lie and say I understand why you ever considered forgiving that rotten cheat, but that's your choice, not mine. I hope you know what you're doing."

She wrapped her arms around my neck. "I told Ray you'd be okay with whatever I wanted, that we didn't have to go through with his crazy plan, but you know how Ray doesn't like to let go of an idea."

I wasn't sure how she got to I'd be okay with what she wanted, but that's Lily. She had a tendency to twist things in her favor. But I loved her anyway, I reminded myself. "Ready for my new creation?"

"As soon as I get out of this black skirt and jacket." She grabbed her big, flowery tote and headed to my bathroom.

"Okay. Meet you in the kitchen." Changing out of my uncomfortable dress-up clothes sounded like the best idea I'd heard all morning and that bar was pretty darn low. I went into my bedroom, unzipped my little black dress, and let it fall around my ankles. Slipping on my favorite tan capris and a white, soft-as-bunny-ears t-shirt, I felt almost normal again. With a quick finger comb through my unruly auburn curls, I pulled it into a ponytail and twisted it into my version of a messy bun which did wonders for making me feel like a new woman. One who was ready to try and figure out what else Lily Lemay might have overlooked telling me. Not on purpose, of course. But I didn't doubt that something had slipped her mind with all the stress and drama of Ray Lemay's fake funeral.

Lily was still in the bathroom when I walked by on my way to the kitchen. I could hear her talking. To Ray? I shook my head. What she saw in that guy was beyond me, always was, and always would be.

I put a bacon, egg, and cheese corn muffins on a plate. One of my latest projects. I figured all the fishermen would love to take their egg breakfast onboard, so why not put all the best ingredients together in a corn muffin—extra-large, of course. After a bit of tweaking, I was pretty happy with the result, but I could never have enough guinea pigs try out my creations first before selling something new at the diner.

"Here you go, Lil." I handed the warmed-up extravaganza to her after she finally hung up and joined me. "Anything new with Ray?" I raised my eyebrows for emphasis.

Pink bloomed in her cheeks but she didn't answer my question. No problem, I got my point across. She bit into the muffin. "This is fantastic, Dani. Are we selling these?"

"Tomorrow morning, and I expect they'll fly out the door before the sun is even up." I loved creating new and somewhat unusual combinations for my loyal fishing customers. They needed something easy, hearty, and delicious to go with their gallons of coffee.

I sat across from Lily. "Now that you're maybe getting back together with Ray, are you still planning to work in the diner? Or, do I have to advertise for help?" I couldn't help but wonder if our workplace balance was about to shift because of this whole sordid plan.

The bloom in Lily's cheeks had returned, telling me she'd recovered from the shock of the fake funeral and the stress of 'fessing up to me. "Of course, I'll still be working," she said with one of her smiles that could light the night sky. "One of the conditions I told Ray was that I wasn't, under any circumstance, going to just hang around the house waiting on him all the time. I was putting myself first this time and doing what I want." Lily grinned. "Aren't you proud of me for that?"

"Yes, that's great." And I meant it except for the part where I could tell Ray would now be hanging around the diner all the time making a nuisance of himself while Lily worked. I sighed. I'd figure something out. "Is it time to head downstairs to meet Ray?"

"You're coming too?" A look of horror filled her face.

"Well, yeah. You think I'm going to let you face that slippery guy on your own? He already involved you in one ridiculous plan today. I think you need some backup, so you don't agree to another one. But don't worry, I'll keep my mouth shut and let you do the talking."

"Okay. You're right. We could talk outside if he insists on privacy." She washed down the last of her muffin with the rest of her blueberry cordial and stood up.

I led the way through my small apartment, down the stairs, and to the kitchen entrance of the Little Dog Diner.

The door was partially open. "Darn. I must not have pulled it tight when I grabbed the cordial." I pushed it open the rest of the way and held my arm out to usher her through. "After you, Lil."

She walked inside and before I even lifted my foot onto the doorsill, an ear-piercing scream filled the kitchen.

Lily crumpled to the floor.

What now? I hoped it didn't have anything to do with my blueberry cordial.

My eyes scanned the kitchen, but my brain had trouble comprehending the scene. Flour covered everything. Papers were strewn about. Drawers hung open with silverware spilled onto the floor. The biggest surprise though, was Ray stretched out on the floor. My blood boiled. I poked him with my foot. "Get up, Ray. That stupid trick only works once."

He didn't move.

As a matter of fact, I noticed that his face was as white as the flour dusted all over the kitchen with a crimson puddle under his head. This was no fake death; it looked like the real thing this time.

My stomach, having a very difficult morning, almost heaved up the blueberry cordial.

With my feet frozen in place, the only thing that moved was my head, surveying everything again, not believing the horror of a ransacked, destroyed, ripped apart kitchen. My kitchen. Where I created recipes and tweaked them until they were perfect. My sanctuary. A rage flooded through me. Whoever did this, messed with the wrong person.

And then I saw Ray's little terrier, Pip, cowering under the table, her dark eyes peering through flour-covered hair as if she was trying to tell me to save her from whatever fate had befallen her master.

My first thought should have been to worry about Ray, but to be honest, I didn't care one bit about him. All thoughts of my destroyed kitchen also left me. Instead, I wondered what would happen to Pip. She already had endured a terrible trauma by the time Ray found her starving, terrified, and bedraggled, wandering the beach after a storm. When no owner ever appeared, Ray took Pip in. I had to admit, that was one quality I had admired about him. The only one.

My heart nearly broke in two looking at that petrified little face that seemed to beg me to rescue her.

I promised I would.

CHAPTER THREE

L ily's eyes fluttered as she groaned on the floor.

Pip dashed to her side and promptly licked her face from her brows to her chin. This scene was getting old in my opinion. With Pip's pink lopsided bow flopping around her ears, she danced around Lily, having suddenly regained her usual hyper, canine self.

I pulled myself together enough to call 911 and say there was an emergency at the Little Dog Diner before I hung up.

Calling this an emergency was probably an understatement, but it was all I could manage with Lily on the floor and Pip turning into a four-legged whirlwind of happiness around her.

I reached toward Lily, helping to pull her upright.

My attention returned to my surroundings. Ray lay sprawled in the center of our totally destroyed kitchen. Or his body lay sprawled in front of me, but Ray had moved on to wherever shady real estate scammers go after they depart this earth.

"Did Ray destroy the kitchen out of some kind of revenge for you leaving the funeral with me?" I asked Lily, "and then he slipped and knocked his head on something?"

Lily turned away from my gaze. Great, there must be something else she hadn't told me. I was beginning to think there were some serious cracks in this friendship of ours.

"Lily? Why do you think Ray wanted to meet you here?" Little fingers of fear creepy crawled up my spine.

And then I saw my cherry rolling pin on the floor next to Ray. The rich reddish wood with streaks of dark brown swirling through it had been a gift from Rose, eleven years ago, when I turned sixteen. I loved that rolling pin. It made the best piecrusts — flakey and light. But now? Something, that looked eerily like blood was smeared on one end along with bits of something else. I bent closer to look. Hair?

I gave myself a moment to think, which paid off when I discovered the big, bloody dent in Ray's head right above his ear where a chunk of his hair was also missing. He hadn't done that to himself.

I dragged myself up off my knees, ran outside and heaved a blue mess behind the trash can next to the kitchen door. Then I drew in big gulps of fresh air as I sagged against the doorframe. I'd never be able to use that rolling pin again.

A yapping sound drew my attention to my ankles, where I discovered Pip. She had followed me out, though if she was similarly distressed by the state of her master's body, I couldn't tell. She shook her little flour-covered body, releasing a white cloud that slowly settled around us. Her sweet face was a stark contrast to the scene in the Little Dog Diner's kitchen, and I couldn't help but smile at her before my brain replayed the scene inside. No matter how many times I ran it over in my mind, I couldn't come up with any explanation except foul play.

Ray dead was one thing…but murdered?

The whine of sirens brought me to my senses, and I gave Pip a quick swipe to dust more flour off her head before I called, "Lily?" and headed back into the diner.

She had some explaining to do, and I wanted to hear what she had to say before the emergency responders got any closer. I grabbed Pip, and cradled the little terrier in my arms so she wouldn't contaminate the crime scene any more than she already had, and went back inside.

"Lily!" I called again, this time louder and with much less patience.

I stood about a foot away from Ray's body, not sure what to do. This felt way too creepy. Where was Lily?

"Danielle Mackenzie?"

I turned at the sound of a familiar, deep rumbling voice. "AJ?" I said, turning around in surprise as the body attached to the voice walked through the front door of the diner and gave the scene a cursory once over.

"You called in the emergency?" he asked.

I pointed to Ray, for the second time in recent history, unable to speak. AJ glanced down at Ray. His eyes popped and I know he swallowed hard because I saw his Adam's apple bobbing. "Noooo," I heard him mutter.

I looked at Ray, then back to Detective AJ Crenshaw, wishing for a moment I could turn back the clock. "Yes," I said reluctantly, not because I was feeling remorse about Ray's demise. I was thinking, poor AJ. This had to be devastating for him. The detective and Ray had been best friends since they both got busted for stealing penny candy at the Misty Harbor Market when they were tweens.

"What happened?" he asked, trying to hide his shock behind his professional demeanor. He reached into his coat pocket, a shiny blue windbreaker that had seen better days, and pulled out a note pad and pen. I'm not sure he was in full detective mode or just needed something to do with his hands.

"All I know is that Ray wanted to meet Lily here. When we came down from my apartment," I waved my arm in an arc, "this...this utter chaos is what we found."

"We? Where's Lily?" Detective Crenshaw fixed me with a stare that nailed me to the wall. "Looks to me like you're the only one here, Danielle." He knelt over the rolling pin, tapped it with a pencil and then moved Ray's hair aside with the same pencil to examine the dent in Ray's head. The dark look he shot me gave me goose bumps. "The murder weapon," he declared.

His lips pursed into a thin line. He meant business, like he was ready to charge the first person he came across with his friend's death.

I glared back at him. I hated it when anyone called me Danielle. It reminded me of every time I got in trouble and my mother said 'Danielle Rose Mackenzie' as if saying my full name was the biggest insult she could bestow upon me. In her mind, it probably was, since she hated that my father won the battle of naming me after his mother—Rose Mackenzie. Those two women couldn't get along if their life depended on it.

"I'm not sure," I said, suddenly feeling like there was no air in the room. "After we discovered the body, I knew I was going to lose my breakfast." Thinking about it made me weak in the knees. "I rushed outside, making it just in time before I threw up, and when I came back inside, Lily was gone." I was just as curious about Lily's whereabouts as the detective was, but probably for very different reasons.

He took my arm, gently, and guided me toward the door. "I'll have to secure this building and you'll have to wait outside."

At least that was a relief. Getting away from Ray's body couldn't happen quickly enough to suit me. I stepped back into the sunshine and fresh air, with half the town of Misty Harbor gawking at the diner. News sure does travel when it has a hint of scandal attached to it. Then I saw a big straw hat you'd never forget and a face that has always made everything better for me. I fell straight into the open arms of my grandmother.

"Oh, Rose …" That was all I could manage before I sagged into her embrace. Her familiar patchouli scent both calmed and soothed me.

My grandmother, Rose to everyone, including me, had been a dominant force in my life ever since my dad died when I was sixteen and my mom decided she had other plans and they didn't include hanging around Misty Harbor, raising a daughter and fighting with her mother-in-law. I guess I should have been bitter, but truth be told, I'm sure I ended up with the better deal in the bargain. Maybe Mom knew that, too, as she drifted in and out of my life.

Rose took me in and never looked back. She didn't ever let me think I'd been abandoned. To her, I was the daughter she'd always wanted and surrounded me with her unconditional love. Tough sometimes and unbending, but always, always with my best interest in mind.

"What's going on, Dani?" she asked in her special soft, we'll-get-through-this-together voice. "I was right next door in my office, and I heard the sirens."

I sniffled and wiped away a tear with my shoulder. "Ray Lemay is inside…dead."

Why was I crying? I didn't like the guy. I didn't mourn him. But, oh, the way he died. The horror that somebody murdered him. I tried but I just couldn't keep it together.

Rose pushed me far enough away so she could look into my eyes and whispered. "An accident, right?" An unmistakably hopeful ring laced her question.

I shook my head because I couldn't utter another word just then, not even a *no*.

She leaned close to my ear. "You didn't kill him, did you? For pulling that ridiculous prank on Lily?"

I could feel my eyes pop open. The hits just kept coming. "You know about that?" Had that fake funeral already made the rounds through Misty Harbor? Did someone decide they preferred the dead Ray Lemay to the live one?

Rose straightened her straw hat. "Of course, I

know. It's my job to know everything that goes on in this town. You know that, Dani. How else could I keep the Blueberry Bay Grapevine filled with enough news to get people to actually read it in the age of the Internet? I write articles they can't find anywhere else. So, answer my question...*did* you kill him?" She mouthed the question since more and more people were crowding around the outside of the Little Dog Diner.

The yellow police tape probably wasn't going to be good for business.

I had started to regain my composure. I shifted Pip in my arms and stood a little taller. "Of course I didn't, Rose. Just because I couldn't stand him, murder isn't exactly my style. Especially not with my favorite cherry rolling pin."

Rose's mouth dropped open. "The one I gave you? That belonged to my mother before I gave it to you. That's the murder weapon? Someone will pay for this."

Her question and answer dialogue shot out faster than I could squeeze in an answer. The outrage in her voice barely matched the enraged expression on her face—clamped jaw, eyes the color of a dark storm cloud, all of it spoke to a determination to get to the bottom of this no matter what

—I knew that expression from my ten years of living with Rose.

I leaned in with a question of my own. "Did *you*?"

I had to ask because, as much as I didn't like Ray, Rose had a problem with him, too. Frankly, she didn't have much use for the whole Lemay clan. It went way back, to the time Ray's grandfather snubbed her at the altar. Why she stayed in town, I'll never know, but I always guessed that she wanted to make life miserable for him. And that she did.

Rose graced me with her I-won't-even-grant-you-with-an-answer, glare, which I also knew well. "Don't be silly," she said indignantly. "I was working in my office on an article about that ridiculous fake funeral."

Interesting answer. She didn't exactly deny murdering him, and she was right next door at the time of the assault. The Little Dog Diner and her building that housed the Blueberry Bay Grapevine were barely a car width apart. The building that Lily had just told me she wanted to buy. My heart fell into my toes at the direction my thoughts were taking me. Motive and opportunity.

Pip had had enough of my clutching her for

dear life and wiggled out of my arms on to the ground. She looked at me, and I swear, she laughed before she dashed under the yellow police tape, despite my calls for her to stop. The last thing I saw was her little tail wagging as it disappeared inside the diner.

Pip had a mind of her own.

She'd fit right in with Rose and me.

CHAPTER FOUR

Detective AJ Crenshaw stomped out of the Little Dog Diner crime scene with Pip in his arms. Her pink tongue swiped a path from his chin to his cheek before he could turn away from her reach.

"Danielle!" AJ plopped Pip unceremoniously into my arms as if she had a contagious disease. "Control your dog!" he demanded.

I gave her a snuggle and said in her defense, "Apparently you forgot, but this adorable girl is… was…Ray's dog. She *only* wants to stay near him." I gave AJ the most pathetic look I could manage. Inside, I cringed at the thought that I had to defend this cute Jack Russell terrier before AJ decided to send her to the pound or something worse. "And, of course, I'll take charge of her." I hugged her close. "That's exactly what Lily asked me to do."

Okay, that was a little white lie, but Lily, who was officially Pip's owner, now, wasn't around to correct me. She knew I was a sucker for just about any type of animal, and I knew that's what she *would* have said.

If she hadn't flown the coop.

"Well … whatever," AJ muttered. "*You* keep her then. Away from my crime scene," he added for emphasis. Then he lowered his voice so all the town folks milling around couldn't hear him. "And, don't leave town."

That was an odd thing to say to someone who called this small-town home. Where did he think I might dash off to, Timbuktu? "What are you saying, Detective? Am I a suspect?"

"Of course you are. At this point, you and Lily, by your own admission, were at the scene of the crime. If you know where Lily is, tell her she'd better come see me soon…to answer questions about an unusual financial transaction."

"What transaction are you talking about?" I decided to play coy. How could he know about the payoff? Who knows, maybe there was more than one.

AJ's face had taken on a reddish hue; evidently investigating a crime scene is hard work. "I'm sure your friend told you about the large sum of money Ray planned to deposit in an account for her."

I feigned surprise. "So what's wrong with that? Lily's husband isn't allowed to give her money?"

The fact that AJ already knew about the transaction shocked me, but I certainly wasn't going to let him know that.

AJ took hold of my arm and pulled me away from the crowd. I took Rose's arm and pulled her along with us. Pip had no choice but to be part of this cozy group.

From the stern look on AJ's face, you'd never know we had a long history going back to grade school. "The timing is suspect," he snarled, "and don't try to tell me otherwise. Ray told me all about Lily's money demands. He wanted my advice about whether he was doing the right thing or not. For some crazy reason, he had convinced himself that he couldn't live without her."

"What did you tell him?" Rose asked, her straw hat flapping in the light breeze that came up.

A look of confusion grew on AJ's face. "There was only one answer to that question in my opinion —no! What on earth possessed Ray to even consider a deal like that? If Ray had to pay Lily to come back to him, there wasn't much hope for a real reconciliation. Surely, you can see that too, Dani. Make sure you let Lily know she has some questions to answer." He stomped back inside and closed the door this time. No more chance of Pip messing up the crime scene.

"Come on Dani." Rose had her arm tucked through mine as we headed toward her office. I was still in shock about this whole money transfer thing. AJ was right, of course, even if I'd never tell him that. Something smelled fishy about this money arrangement, and I couldn't figure out what Lily was up to. Why did she all of a sudden, out of the blue, think she needed to own *this* building?

"Hey Dani," someone in the crowd shouted. "Did your chowdah kill someone?" Everyone laughed.

I turned around and locked my eyes on the person I thought had yelled the insult. "For your information, Joe, I seem to recall that you had some yesterday. How are *you* feeling?"

Maybe it was the light, but it looked like his face took on a green tint.

More laughter filled the air but at least it wasn't directed at me this time. Rose got me moving again.

"Don't let them ruffle your feathers, Dani. Ignore those comments."

Just as we arrived at the Blueberry Bay Grapevine office door, an old pickup truck pulled to a stop. "That must be Spencer with my blueberry delivery," I said as a tailpipe disgorged a cloud of blue smoke. "What am I going to do now? I have no place to store blueberries with the diner locked up tight."

Was she going to ask me to help out? I imagined my little apartment crammed full of blueberries. Maybe I would have to start a new decorating trend.

Rose released my arm and marched over to the truck. She stuck her head in the driver side window while I whispered to Pip. "You and I are going to be a great team. I can tell." I fastened her pink bow on her head, and she licked my chin. "You're very welcome, Pip. I've got the feeling you want to be sure no one mistakes you for a male. Am I right?"

Another lick made me think Pip actually understood what I was saying. It was nice to think that someone, even if that someone was a Jack Russell terrier—a bundle of dynamite packed into a neat little package—agreed with me. I let myself into Rose's office while she solved the blueberry storage dilemma. Dealing with the Little Dog Diner orders, deliveries, and any associated problems was her responsibility.

I put Pip down, found a small bowl, and gave her some water. After she sniffed around the room, she helped herself to a drink. I took one of Rose's old sweaters and made a nest on a chair, patting it so Pip knew she had a comfy place to curl up when she was ready.

Rose's office had one of those coffee machines that made single servings, so I fiddled with a pod until a stream of hot French roast filled my cup, and then I walked to the front window to see what was taking Rose so long. She stood next to the Blueberry Acres delivery truck with her arm on the open passenger window and the growing Misty Harbor crowd of gawkers staring them down. I guess I couldn't blame them. Our little town had never had an event that was this gory. Not by a long shot.

As the driver unfolded himself from the truck, my mug of hot coffee shook and *almost* slipped out of my hand.

"What are *you* doing here?" I asked the empty room, too shocked at the sight of Luke Sinclair heading up the walkway with his arm linked with

Rose's. Luke, who left town eight years ago – taking my heart with him.

With a smile pasted on my face to cover up the total upheaval of my emotions, I opened the door to let them in.

"What a surprise," I said. The words sounded almost normal, if you ignored the dash of scorn that slipped into my tone.

"Dani?" Luke blinked as he said it with what I could only imagine was disbelief. Over Luke's shoulder, Rose graced me with a, you'll-thank-me-later smile. Apparently, she hadn't told him I was in her office, preferring to blindside both of us. What was she up to?

"Luke's come home to help his dad," she said. "Did I forget to tell you that, Dani? He's got some great new ideas to bring more customers to their blueberry farm. We've been brainstorming a bit, so I can promote the events in the Grapevine— pancake breakfast, wagon rides around the farm, pet photos—it's just the beginning."

I stood in shock, knowing my mouth was hanging open, barely hearing Rose's chatter. All that registered was that somehow Luke was more handsome than I remembered with his deep tan, a few smile wrinkles, his hair swept casually back and his body toned and muscular. With his mouth turned up into a smile, nothing had changed about the deep blue eyes that stared at me as if he could read my thoughts. "Hi, Dani. Good to see you."

"You're back. For more than a few days?" For the life of me, I couldn't get the snark out of my voice, but who could blame me?

Luke had an aw shucks smile that didn't fit the picture I had of his life since he left Misty Harbor. "It looks like it," he said. "Dad can't run the farm by himself anymore, and I couldn't bear that he actually considered selling the property. So," he held his hands out to his sides and raised his eyebrows, "I've decided to keep the farm going and maybe find some work on the side while I'm here."

Rose straightened the papers on her desk and picked up her hobo bag. "How about we go to Sea Breeze, have some lunch, and make a plan?"

By Sea Breeze, she meant her drop-dead gorgeous house on Blueberry Bay.

"A plan?" I was still in a daze from seeing Luke and couldn't think past the fact that he'd moved back to Misty Harbor. Rose acted as if this was all an everyday occurrence—murder, my old flame back in town, and my best friend nowhere to be found.

Rose snapped her finger in front of my face. "A plan about this murder. And, by the way, where's Lily? I saw her scoot out the front door like her hair was on fire."

That brought me back to earth. Lily. Right. Had she fallen off the edge of the earth? I pulled out my phone and called her.

To my surprise, she answered after the first ring. "Dani?"

"Where the heck are you, Lily?" I wanted to tell her more, but not in front of Luke.

"Are you alone?" Why did she sound tense? And a little frantic?

"Yes," I lied. I turned my back on Rose and Luke, lowered my voice, and hoped their hearing wasn't great. "Where are you? Detective Crenshaw wants to talk to you, like, half an hour ago."

"I think I'm in trouble, and I'm afraid to tell you where I am."

If this day got any crazier it would qualify for free tickets at the nearest zoo. "Listen, Lily, the longer you stay away, it looks like you've got something to hide."

Rose sneezed.

"Who was that?" Lily asked. "You said you were alone."

"Just Rose…and Luke Sinclair."

"Luke? He applied for the part time summer deputy job. Don't tell him you're talking to me."

Oh, for crying out loud. Was there a conspiracy against me? "How come everyone in town knows what's going on with Luke except me?" Oops, I sort of raised my voice with that question. I could feel two pairs of eyes burning holes in my back. Pip chose that moment to jump against my leg, which threw me off balance and straight into Luke's chest.

I have to admit, it felt good.

"Dani? Are you still there?" My hand had dropped to my side when I fell. It was no secret to Rose who I was talking to, so she grabbed my phone.

"Lily, listen to me. Meet us at Sea Breeze. Now." Rose said in her no-nonsense mode. "Sheesh," she went on. "Enough of this cloak and dagger stuff. If you're in trouble, you'll need us to help you get out of it." She handed the phone back to me.

I hit the speaker button. Pip was running wild around my feet and I needed to pick her up. "Did you hear all that, Lily? Meet us at Sea Breeze. You know, Rose's house. We're on our way now."

"Okay," she said, giving up the fight. "Dani?" she added before I disconnected the call.

"Yeah?"

"Don't tell them about the money."

"Okay," I said. She didn't know she was on speakerphone so, of course, Rose and Luke could hear what she said for themselves. I kept mum about it, and their confused expressions told me she'd be doing some explaining before too long.

CHAPTER FIVE

Luke left Rose's office first, strolling calmly to his truck and driving away. No one in the crowd that had yet to disperse seemed to take any notice of his old vehicle rattling down the road.

I turned on Rose with my lips pursed, barely controlling my anger. "Why didn't you tell me that Luke was back in town?"

Rose took my arm and led me out the door and around the side of the building to her car. Pip, tucked under my other arm, squirmed and wiggled to get down. "Dani, what difference would it have made? Luke is back and now you know."

She did have a way of putting everything in perspective, but it still rankled me. What *would* I have done? Rushed out to the farm to welcome Luke back with open arms? Of course not!

"What about his wife?" I asked. "I bet *she's* not too keen about living in this small town after the excitement of San Francisco. And on a *farm* no less."

Rose stopped dead in her tracks, pulling me up short, too. "Are you belittling the blueberry farm that we depend on for just about all of your sweet recipes?" She looked at me over her glasses. A look that only meant one thing—think before you let stupid words leave your mouth.

I opened the back door of her old Cadillac, letting Pip have the comfy seat for herself while I slid into the passenger seat, fuming at Rose's rebuke. I waited for Rose to get in and close her door. "I'm not saying that at all. Don't put words in my mouth. I'm just saying that someone like Jennifer, who is used to living in a city with her interest in art galleries and shows and all the glitz and glitter, probably won't enjoy the peace and natural beauty found on a farm." Like I would, I added to myself.

Rose took off her wide-brimmed straw hat and turned to lay it carefully on the back seat. When she eyed Pip and calculated the chances of the terrier chewing it up for an afternoon snack, she plopped it in my lap and said, "Hold this for me." She turned the key and her Caddy fired up with a roar. "And, how do you know all that about Luke and his wife?" Her syrupy voice told me she was about to drop some unwelcome piece of information on me. The Caddy rumbled as she put it in gear, as if her precious car was in cahoots by adding a big exclamation point at the end of her words.

I crossed my arms and clamped my lips together. I was not giving an inch on this. Surely, Rose hadn't forgotten my heartache over Luke.

"For your information, whoever has been feeding you information about Luke, is behind the times. He's divorced."

And just like that, my heart beat with a glimmer of hope that whatever it was that Luke and I had in the past might have a chance to rekindle. Not that I had my hopes up too high. He'd left and shattered my heart once, and I wasn't going to let it happen again.

Before I had a chance to ask her for details on Luke's new life, Rose changed the subject. "Tell me, Dani. What did Lily mean when she said 'don't tell them about the money'? AJ mentioned a money transfer. Is that connected?"

I looked out the window instead of at Rose. We

were outside the downtown mix of crafty shops, old homes, and tourists bustling along the narrow streets. She drove along the curvy Oceanside Road giving me random glimpses of Blueberry Bay glistening beyond the rocky coastline. My breathing settled into a normal rhythm.

"I'll tell you what I know when we get to Sea Breeze. There's no point in telling it twice. And, to be honest, I don't know much. Lily has the story and, so far, she hasn't shared much with me."

I turned and studied Rose's profile—rigid with concern I decided. "Where are you going to store the blueberries?"

"That's a huge problem for Luke."

"Really? Aren't we sort of responsible for helping him out with that?"

Rose reached across the wide front seat and held my hand. Her warmth and strength traveled straight to my heart. Even when we quarreled, we never stayed upset with each other for long. "That's not what I meant. Luke already unloaded the berries into the walk-in freezer at the diner. He had his dad's key to let himself in."

"Oh," I said and smiled at her, relieved at least one issue was off the table. "No problem then." As soon as the words left my lips, the meaning behind her statement hit me. "He was in the diner *this* morning?" A cold chill raised goosebumps along my arms.

Now I saw a determined line around her mouth. "Uh huh," she said, confirming my worst suspicion.

"Who else knows he was inside?" My first instinct was to bury this information as deep as possible.

"It's not something he can lie about, Dani." Rose's voice came out soft and heavy with worry. "Luke left the invoice with the date of delivery written in his own handwriting. It won't take AJ more than an eye blink to put two and two together. Talking to Luke will be high on his agenda. That's why I suggested Luke come to my house before going home. It gives him a breather before the storm hits on the farm."

I didn't know what to make of this latest twist. Pip whined in the back seat as if she understood my worry. She jumped over the front seat and pushed herself under Rose's hat where she curled up on my lap. "Quite a morning for you, little girl," I murmured taking in the events for myself as I stroked her head which poked out from under one side of the hat.

"What's your plan for Pip?" Rose asked as she pulled between the two granite pillars that marked her driveway.

"Well, Lily, goodhearted though she is, really isn't a dog person. And poor Pip already had one traumatic chapter in her life by the time Ray found her wandering on the beach—drenched, starving, and near death—and who knows what happened this morning at the Little Dog Diner, I think, if she'll have me, I'll share my life with her."

I looked at Rose, hoping she agreed with my decision, but if she didn't, it wouldn't change my mind one bit because it was already made up.

Rose hit the button to open her garage door and pulled inside.

Pip raised her head and looked at me. I felt a shiver run through her little body. "Don't worry, Pip, I won't let anything happen to you."

Rose turned the car off and shifted in the seat until she faced me. "I like to pride myself on my ability to anticipate what's happening in this town. But I have to say, this morning came as a shock of all shocks. But, one thing I'm sure of, you and Pip are absolutely right for each other."

She reached over and scratched under Pip's ear. Her little tongue came out and licked Rose's fingers.

My heart soared. It wasn't often that Rose ever told me that anything was absolutely right, so I had to be sure that Pip and I didn't let her down. The only other time she'd told me something was absolutely right for me was when I brought Luke to meet her after our first date. She told me, "Dani, that boy will make your heart sing and your feet fly."

She sure got that wrong! He left town and made my heart crack into a million pieces, and my feet get sucked into the mud.

I hugged Pip and decided I'd settle for her unconditional love instead.

CHAPTER SIX

Rose owned Sea Breeze, a shingled and wind-swept two-story, many-bedroomed house of memories on a point of land that had one side of her house facing Blueberry Bay and the other side sheltered under towering pines. It had been my home for ten years, since I was sixteen until I moved to the apartment in town a year ago. Pip and I followed Rose from the garage through to the kitchen to find Luke and the teakettle whistling. That didn't mean much I told myself, anyone could boil water, but it was a sweet gesture. One tiny crack in my heart mended when I smelled mint tea steeping. He had remembered one of my favorites.

His smile, when he turned at the sound of our footsteps, crinkled the edges of his eyes and mended another tiny crack. I was in deep trouble with Luke Sinclair back in Misty Harbor.

"Rose, I hope you don't mind that I raided your fridge and made us lobster rolls for lunch." Luke set a tray on the counter with plump rolls spilling pink lobster meat over the sides. My stomach growled and my mouth watered in anticipation. I wasn't used to a handsome man serving me lunch on a warm summer day. It felt better than a soak in a hot tub.

Pip's nails clicked on the tiled floor as she danced around my legs. I snuck a loose piece of lobster to her and she politely sniffed it before licking it off my fingers. She looked up at me, telegraphing a *more please* expression, and I imagined it cemented the new bond between us.

Luke crouched down in front of Pip. "Here you go," he said, pulling a small dog bone from his pocket. He held it out and Pip just about lost her mind jumping for it. "She might like this better," he said to me with the grin that used to melt my heart.

She took the bone daintily between her front teeth and went to work on it. Luke ruffled her ears and added, "I always keep a few in my pocket for the dogs I meet on my deliveries."

Luke had always been a softy when it came to

animals, collecting all sorts of injured creatures and giving them a second chance. Should I think he might give my injured heart a second chance, too? Get a grip, Dani, I told myself. Forget about romance. There are more important things happening—a murder to solve for instance.

"Dani? What is it with you today?" Rose touched my arm, and looked at me with concern, snapping me away from my nostalgic memories and hopeful fantasies. "You can't seem to stay focused for more time than it takes for a wave to crash on the beach. Grab some glasses, the pitcher of water, and the pot of tea. We're going to sit on the patio, enjoy our lobster rolls, the sound of the tide rolling in, and the scent of the sea breeze."

I could manage that, I told myself.

Once we were all settled, Rose pinned me with her look. "It's time for you to tell us what Lily meant about the money she didn't want us to know about."

I took a bite of my lobster roll, buying time to replay my earlier conversation with Lily. "Delicious lunch." I wiped the edge of my mouth with the back of my hand, shifted in my seat, and let out a deep sigh. "Something's going on that smells like rotten eggs and it didn't start with Ray's fake funeral."

Luke choked and pounded on his chest. It looked like he got his napkin in front of his mouth just in time to avoid an embarrassing spray of food. "I thought Ray was murdered," he managed to mumble after his coughing fit subsided.

"Oh, he was," I said. "The fake funeral happened *before* someone murdered him in the kitchen of the Little Dog Diner."

Luke shook his head. He must have been trying to dislodge this craziness before he asked any more questions. "I know Ray was always into drama in a big way but a fake funeral? That seems a bit much even for him."

I sank back into Rose's expensive patio chair and crossed one leg over the other. "What Lily said is that they planned a reconciliation and the fake funeral was somehow supposed to convince his family that Lily really did still love him. Lily bringing me along was an added prop."

"And the money?" Rose asked, adjusting her ever-present straw hat and getting me back on track with her original question.

"The money was an incentive to get back in Lily's good graces." I sipped my mint tea not convinced it was the best beverage for a warm summer day.

"Oh, my lord." Rose stared across the bay. "Buying someone's affection can't be a good idea for a successful marriage on *any* level."

"That's what I told Lily. Plus, Ray wanted her to make an offer to buy your building. He knew you'd never sell to *him*." I was probably imagining it, but it sure looked like Rose's pupils turned as dark as a raging nor'easter in the middle of January.

"I'll wait for Lily to explain all that," she replied in what sounded to be a calm voice. But I knew Rose and I knew something was brewing underneath that calm exterior. And, I was glad I wouldn't be the target.

We heard a car door slam. Pip, who had been sitting in the shade of my chair, charged along the stone path leading to the front of the house. "I hope that's Lily, come to her senses." I didn't hold out much hope for that, though, after the morning craziness.

Pip, with her head high and prancing like a little princess, led Lily to us. My best friend, on the other hand, dragged her feet, and hung her head. I could only imagine the embarrassment she must be feeling—something like facing a firing squad.

Rose, to her credit, embraced Lily like she was a wounded robin in need of some tender loving care. Her multi colored skirt blew in the breeze and she had to clamp her hand on her straw hat to keep it from cartwheeling away. "Come and sit with us, dear. Are you hungry? You must be. Would you like a lobster roll? Of course, you would."

Rose's rapid-fire questions and answers gave Lily no chance to respond. Her lip quivered when she glanced in my direction but with her eyes hidden behind dark glasses, I couldn't tell what she was thinking. She had no idea that Rose was making her comfy so she could come in for the kill.

Rose pulled a fourth chair next to mine, opened a big umbrella to shade us, and set a plate with a lobster roll in Lily's lap.

"Before you all start to shoot questions at me, there are a couple of things I have to say." Lily slid off her sunglasses, swallowed, and pulled her long blonde braid over her shoulder. Her habit when she was nervous.

We waited.

"I didn't kill Ray."

"Of course you didn't," I said. "You were with me in my apartment." I couldn't help but wonder if there was any sliver of chance that she had time to slip down to the diner while I was in my room changing, but I kept that thought to myself.

"Besides that," Lily continued, "I had no intention of trying to buy Rose's building. I only wanted Ray's money so I wouldn't have to rely on some sort of allowance from him." She looked at me. "I knew you'd tell them about the money, Dani."

"Why did Ray want my building, Lily?" Rose asked. She kept her voice neutral even though I knew she must have been fuming inside.

She shrugged. "I'm not sure, but he floated the idea about an upscale restaurant in a prime location." I couldn't miss the blush that crept over her cheeks. "He thought I should be managing a fancier restaurant that would cater to the tourists instead of," Lily made finger quotes, "'the dumb diner that the locals go to'—Ray's words. He thought your building would be perfect for what he was planning."

I jumped to my feet ready to kill someone. The only problem was that the subject of my anger was already dead. "What? That slime ball insulted our diner? Everyone in town loves our breakfast and lunch food. Who does he think he is?"

Rose patted my arm. "Don't forget that Ray is dead. He can't follow through on any of his plans now, Dani. *My* question is," she pinpointed her glare on Lily, "why did *you* go along with his scheme?"

"I really wanted to give our marriage another chance. I know you think I'm foolish but, well, I just did. I didn't want our new beginning to start with a big fight. I planned to work on changing his mind over time." She looked away from all of us. Part of me felt sorry that she'd never get a second chance with Ray, but the other part of me was thrilled she wouldn't get that second chance. I knew that didn't make any sense, but in my heart, I knew Lily was better off *without* Ray in her life.

My internal debate almost made me miss Lily's next statement.

"…and, I think my life is in danger. That's why I took off when we found Ray dead on the floor in the diner. I panicked, Dani. I just lost my common sense and took off."

My hand darted to Lily and grabbed hers. With both hands, I pulled it to my chest. "What are you talking about? What kind of danger?" All my frustration with her evaporated in that millisecond of concern for her safety.

Rose poured a glass of ice water from a pitcher on the patio table and handed it to Lily. "Drink this and then tell us what's going on. This story gets more mixed up by the minute."

Luke, who had been sitting silently while the three of us aired our woes, stood up and paced across the patio. It was obvious to me that something was bothering him, but I assumed he was concerned about what Lily just told us. Luke, to his credit, had more empathy than most men I knew.

"There's something I probably should tell you that fills a gap in Lily's story," Luke said. He had finally settled back in his chair and planted his elbows on his knees. He barely got any words out with his jaw clenched so tightly. I sure hoped he wasn't about to confess that he'd bludgeoned Ray Lemay over the head. I might be able to forgive him for the murder but not for desecrating my beloved cherry rolling pin.

All eyes were on Luke.

"Here's the thing," he began. "I found out that Ray was behind the person putting the pressure on my dad to sell Blueberry Acres. I had a shouting match with Ray … in the town square … with plenty of witnesses."

Rose flicked her wrist dismissively. "I saw that. It means nothing. Of course you were upset. It's not like you attacked him physically."

Luke raised his hand to stop her. "True, but with me being at the diner this morning to deliver your blueberries, it puts me at the scene of the crime. It won't take much for people to make the leap and assume I might have killed Ray to stop him from helping someone buy the farm. If I were anyone else, I'd see it as a pretty strong motive."

My heart sank when I saw the despair and worry etched on Luke's face. Did I think he killed Ray Lemay? Not really, but hadn't I just had murderous thoughts myself? Sometimes things happen in the heat of the moment.

Ray brought out those deadly reactions in many people.

The question was, who else would like to see Ray dead?

CHAPTER SEVEN

Luke left us with our half-eaten lobster rolls and anxiety-filled thoughts. At least, that's how I felt. Sitting on Rose's patio with Blueberry Bay stretched in front of us should have been a relaxing way to spend a summer afternoon, but with Lily spilling her guts to us, the day couldn't end soon enough.

Rose gathered up the plates. "I'm taking this inside before the seagulls swoop in and help themselves. I really don't want to encourage that kind of visitor to my patio. Come on Pip, I'll fix something for you, too."

"Here's the thing," Lily said when it was just the two of us and the view, "Ray confessed to me that he had some shady clients looking for prime real estate. The trouble started when he promised he could deliver a piece of property on the Bay to get them to buy a worthless piece of unbuildable property he had to unload. I don't know what he was thinking, because he knew he couldn't deliver the waterfront land. He didn't seem to think there would be any consequences."

"Let me guess," I said, "Ray needed Rose's building and the blueberry farm to make those creeps happy."

"Something like that. He was hoping that might solve his problem. It was his idea to transfer money to an account in my name, so he didn't lose everything if things went off the rails. I was only trying to help, but now I'm afraid whoever killed Ray might be after me next." She dropped her face into her hands. "I don't know what to do. I'm sure the police will want to question me, right?" When Lily looked up at me, her eyes were filled with a heartbreaking mixture of fear and sadness.

I had to tell her the truth. "AJ was adamant about needing to talk to you. He knows about the money transfer, too. But you have an alibi, Lily. You were with me the whole time."

She quirked her eyebrows and then said,

disheartened, "Until I ran out the front door after we found Ray's body."

I gave her snarky grin. "Right. Thanks for leaving me with that mess, but in hindsight, you did the right thing." I tapped my nails on the arm of the chair, trying to come up with a plan. "First, we need to find out who was at the fake funeral. Maybe someone there followed Ray to the diner while we were upstairs. Someone who saw how upset you were and figured they could frame you."

That idea put some color back in her cheeks, and Lily smiled at me. "You really are my best friend, but I don't want to put you in danger, too."

"Danger and Dani do *not* go together. I'll look danger right in the eye and shoo it away."

Lily laughed, which helped to lighten the whole difficult situation. The way I saw it, if I didn't help Lily, who would? "So, you know Ray's family and friends better than I do. Any suspects you can think of?"

"Well, his sister wasn't happy about us getting back together. She wanted a part of the business, and she always resented everything about me."

"Okay, anyone else?"

Lily tapped her finger against her lips. "You know that Ray owns the Two Wilde Funeral Home building, but you probably didn't know that the two brothers, Frank and Nick, have been trying to buy it from him for, like, forever. I never heard that it was moving forward."

"Speaking of them, why did they ever agree to this fake funeral? The whole idea was such a strange thing, and wouldn't it be a blemish on their business?"

"Good question. I never asked Ray about that." A smirk grew on her face. "I'd say we need to make a visit to Frank and Nick with some questions of our own and see how uncomfortable they are. Since I have a real funeral to plan, a visit won't even look suspicious."

"You're taking Ray's death really well, Lil. Considering you were thinking about a reconciliation, I thought you'd be more upset."

"Part of me already saw him as dead because of the whole fake funeral thing and reality hasn't hit me yet, I guess. My feelings for Ray have been all over the place." She gazed out at the ocean before she spoke again. "I wouldn't say this to anyone but you, Dani, but in a way, it's easier for me with Ray dead. I don't have to wonder whether I want to try to repair our difficult relationship … or wonder if he would cheat on me again if we *did* get back together."

"I understand completely and no matter what, Lil, you'll come through this one way or another." I stood up and stretched my arms over my head, twisting my back from side to side to loosen up the stiff muscles. "Now, I'm going into Rose's kitchen to whip up a big batch of blueberry coffee cake. It never hurts to have a tasty bribe when popping in unexpectedly on possible murder suspects. And while I'm taking care of that, you'd better head over to the police station and get AJ off your trail. There's plenty for him to dig into around Ray's business dealings instead of worrying about whether you smashed Ray over the head."

All was good; I had my best friend back. As we headed into the cool house, arm in arm, a little voice in my head said, I hope nothing else comes along to spoil my life.

Then we heard voices and I stopped Lily from going any farther. "Who's Rose talking to?" I asked.

We could hear the faint murmur of Rose's voice and a deeper, male voice. Pip's nails clicked on the tiles as she dashed over and jumped on my legs. I picked her up. Rose had changed her pink bow to purple, her favorite color, but Pip didn't seem to care as she licked my chin.

"There you two are." Rose followed Pip's route with Detective AJ Crenshaw four steps behind.

"Look who dropped by," she said with a roll of her eyes, which only Lily and I could see. "Dani and Lily just finished lunch. Do you want to sit in my living room to talk with the girls? I can make some iced tea in two shakes of a lemon. They've had an extremely difficult morning so I'm sure you won't upset them anymore, Detective."

Rose held her arm out and more or less herded us like kids into her enormous living room—a subtle reminder of her wealth and influence in town. Maybe that was her understated way of telling AJ to be nice to us.

Rose was not a woman to be messed with. She had roots that went back generations, maybe even to the Mayflower, and more real estate in her name than anyone else in town. She usually liked to fly under the radar, but if she needed to remind the detective about her influence in order to protect Lily or me, she wouldn't hesitate.

I wanted to hug her, but that would have to wait until AJ left.

Rose fluttered around like a mother hen, a bossy

hen who wanted everything her way. She told each of us where to sit, choosing the softest, lowest chair for AJ, which made him sink below both Lily and me on the firmer loveseat. I chuckled to myself at her deviousness.

"I'll be right back," she said in a singsong voice that almost made me gag. I hoped she wasn't slathering the fake charm on too thick.

AJ shifted around on the soft cushion, but the more he moved, the more it swallowed up his lower half. His knees were at least six inches higher than his butt, and he looked really uncomfortable. He opened a notebook and clicked a ballpoint pen. "Tell me exactly what happened this morning," he said, trying to insert some authority into his voice.

"Where should we start?" I asked. "From the moment I got out of bed?" With Lily's leg crammed next to mine, I couldn't miss her slight jiggle.

"That won't be necessary, Danielle. How about starting with you walking into the diner."

I shifted forward like I had an exciting story to tell. I guess in a way, I did, except for the ending. "Well, after the shock of seeing Ray alive at his fake funeral," I glanced quickly at Lily, "we left the funeral home and drove to the Little Dog Diner. I grabbed a bottle of my blueberry cordial thinking, if what we'd just witnessed wasn't a good reason to have a sip at ten in the morning, well then, I had no idea what would warrant it."

AJ stuck his pen behind his ear. "Blueberry cordial, huh? Was Ray in the diner then?"

"Of course not! As far as we knew, he was still at the funeral home. We were the first ones out of there when Ray rose up from the dead, or so it seemed." I pointed at AJ. "Maybe you should be asking Frank and Nick Wilde why on earth they ever agreed to that foolish stunt."

"Thank you for the suggestion, Danielle, but I'm here to talk to the two of *you*. You were in the diner with your drink of blueberry cordial. When did Ray arrive?" He pulled his pen out of his hair like some sort of magician.

"You've got that wrong, AJ."

He raised his eyebrows. "That's what you just told me."

"No, I said I grabbed a bottle of blueberry cordial, but I never said we drank it in the diner."

"Where did you drink it?" The frustration in his voice indicated he was just about to boil over. I had to admit, this was kind of fun.

"We went upstairs to my apartment. I live on the second floor of Rose's historic building. You know, above the Blueberry Bay Grapevine." Of course, he knew. Everyone in town knew I worked at the diner and lived above Rose's office. "We had a drink and changed out of those awful black outfits we'd been wearing for Ray's fake funeral." I turned to Lily. "It's kind of ironic, but now you'll have to plan a real funeral for him."

"Danielle?" AJ said to get my attention. "You called in the emergency. When did you find Ray's body?"

"After Lily and I changed, Ray texted Lily to meet her at the diner." I shrugged. "Who knows what that was about, but she said she would meet him, so together we went downstairs."

"You two stayed together the whole time?"

I was sure he thought he had me in some sort of lie. "We stayed together until after we discovered Ray's body. Remember? I told you I went outside to throw up in the bushes and when I came back inside, Lily was gone."

AJ finally decided he had something worthwhile to scribble in his notebook.

Rose returned with a tray of iced tea and set it on the table between his chair and our loveseat. "Here you go, AJ." She handed him a glass that was dripping with condensation.

It slipped through his fingers and soaked his, well, you can imagine! It was all I could do to keep from laughing. Rose, calmly, wiped his pants. I had to excuse myself to go to the bathroom, tugging Lily along with me.

As soon as the door was closed, we both fell against the door with tears streaming down our cheeks we were laughing so hard. "Did you see his face?" I managed to ask. "I thought he was going to pull out his gun and shoot Rose."

"Or you." Lily grabbed the hand towel and wiped the tears off her cheeks. "Oh, man. I couldn't have planned that any better. We'd better get back out there and finish the story so he can get some dry pants on."

Solemnly, we walked back to the living room and sat across from AJ. Pages from his notebook were spread across the coffee table. Apparently, his pants weren't the only thing that got soaked.

"Lily?" AJ asked as if nothing embarrassing had just happened. "Where did you go after Danielle went outside to throw up?"

I squeezed her hand to transfer some confidence. "Tell him, Lily. Tell him how you were afraid your life might be in danger."

"Danielle! Don't coach her. I want Lily to tell me what happened."

"Sorry. It's just that this has been extremely difficult for Lily."

"When I saw Ray on the floor, I panicked. I ran out the front door, got in my car, and drove around. Ray had told me that he had some shady clients and my first thought was that someone followed him and, well, killed him. I was afraid they might come after me next." Lily wiped a tear from her eye.

Good acting, I thought; or was it real?

"Because of the money transfer?" AJ asked.

"That's what I was thinking."

AJ closed his notebook and carefully gathered all the wet pages from the coffee table. "Do you know who that client was?"

Lily shook her head. "I wish I did. It would be easier to protect myself."

I wrapped my arm around her trembling shoulders. For all her bravado she was really scared which made me scared for her. And angry.

Pip jumped into my lap. Now I had Pip *and* Lily to protect.

What were friends for?

CHAPTER EIGHT

Tuesday morning rolled around with me snug in Rose's luxurious guest room. She'd turned my old bedroom into a library, but I didn't miss it as this room had a better view. She made it clear that I wasn't going to stay alone in my apartment so close to a murder scene. The smell of the sea drifted through the open window.

Gazing out the window, across the bay at the bobbing sailboats and morning lobstermen checking their traps, I vowed to myself to dig into this crazy, mixed-up murder. The Little Dog Diner was my future, and I didn't plan to sit still until it was up and running again serving breakfast sandwiches and coffee cake to all the locals.

By the time I padded downstairs, I found Rose

nestled on the love seat. It was no surprise to find her there since her routine was up and at 'em by four-thirty to watch the sun rise over Blueberry Bay while enjoying a strong cup of hazelnut coffee.

"How did you sleep?" she asked me when I shuffled in at the more normal hour of seven.

Pip, curled up in Rose's lap, was the vision of contentment. She lifted her head and did a funny twitch with her lips, which almost looked like a smile. It hadn't taken her long to make herself right at home.

I wandered to the front window to get my dose of the view. "Your guest room has the best bed I've ever slept in and the quiet here is like a soft down comforter. With the steady sound of the waves coming around the point, I drifted off to sleep and slept better than I have in a long time."

"That is a benefit of this spot. Nothing like a steady rhythm to soothe and calm your mind." She held up her mug towards me. "There's coffee in the kitchen, and you can get me a refill while you're at it. Or, if you're hungry we could get breakfast."

I stayed put in front of the window letting my eyes feast on the view. "Do you ever get tired of this?" I asked Rose, ignoring, for the moment, her beverage and food suggestion.

"Never. Having the ocean as a reminder of something bigger, more powerful, and constant is what keeps me humble. I start my day with that view and know that no matter what happens, the ocean will always be there to bring beauty into my life. It's why I could never move away from this spot."

"Unlike my mother," I said. I wasn't exactly upset, but I never did understand my mother's need to get away from Blueberry Bay.

"We all make the choices that work for us, Dani. Are *you* happy here?"

I turned around and sat on the sofa with Rose, folding my legs under me. "I'm like you. I love this town, this bay, everything here, and because of all that, I have to make sure nothing happens to Lily. I'm worried about her."

"I know you are. She made a bad decision when she took that money from Ray. I don't know if she fully understands who he was dealing with."

This comment startled me. "Do you?" Rose knew so much of what went on in Misty Harbor, but did she know the ins and outs of Ray's real estate business, too?

"I don't know all the details, but what I *do* know is that Ray Lemay made too many bad investments, which put him in financial trouble. And when someone is desperate, they do stupid things. I think Ray's bad choices got him killed." She reached over and gripped my hand with her strong fingers. "Don't go doing anything stupid, Dani. Don't get yourself into trouble or make yourself a target for the bad folks around here."

Her strength traveled up my arm. The concern in her voice warmed my heart and the last thing I wanted to do was worry Rose. "Actually, my plan is to make an extra rich blueberry coffee cake. I think a sweet offering to the Wilde brothers might help when I go with Lily to discuss the real funeral for Ray."

What I didn't tell her was that I hoped to find out more about the fake funeral.

Rose laughed. "Don't think you can fool me, missy. I wasn't born yesterday. Your sweet offering is nothing more than a bribe in exchange for answers." She stretched out her legs, Pip jumped off her lap, and Rose stood up. "Let's get that coffee and think about how we can help Lily."

"I expect her to show up any time for coffee and breakfast."

"Perfect." Rose led the way into her kitchen, aglow with the morning sun streaming through her windows. A rainbow danced across the floor as light reflected off a crystal hanging in the window. Wind chimes tinkled outside, a dainty reminder of the almost constant ocean breeze, gentle this morning, but capable of changing quickly, just like life.

Rose filled her coffee mug with the last of what was in the pot. "I'll make a fresh pot since we're expecting company."

"Do you mind if I take a quick jog on the beach? It's just too inviting to ignore."

Rose shooed me out the door. "Enjoy yourself. Don't forget that you left a couple changes of clothes here for an unexpected visit. Smart planning ahead." She grinned at me, especially since it had been Rose's idea to do this smart planning ahead. She never let me forget anything.

Pip trotted behind me like a little shadow. I assumed she was not keen on being left behind or being left alone. That worked for me. "Come on, Pip. The fresh air will do you good, too."

"Wait a minute." Rose rushed over and tied a purple tie-dyed bandana around Pip's neck. "There you go. Now you have your own special running gear, too."

I couldn't help but chuckle as I took the stairs two at a time to make a quick change.

With dark blue running shorts and a white tank top on, I sat on the edge of the bed to tie my running shoes. "Ready, Pipster?"

In reply, she rewarded me with a high-pitched yip. I shook my head at the thought that this little pipsqueak understood a lot more than she probably got credit for. She was one smart little terrier, and I thanked my lucky stars that whoever did Ray in, hadn't hurt this adorable girl.

Once we were outside on the patio, I did a few stretches and lunges to warm up my muscles, then we slow jogged down the wooden steps that led to a narrow strip of beach in front of Sea Breeze. Well, I slow jogged, but Pip raced ahead, barely letting her feet touch the sand on her way to the edge of the water, barking at the waves, but quickly retreating to avoid getting her feet wet.

Seagulls and sandpipers darted ahead of us or took off into the blue sky. I sucked in a lungful of invigorating salty air and let my legs carry me across the sand. "Come on Pip. We should have the beach to ourselves at this time of the morning."

She raced ahead of me with yips and yaps at the birds that brazenly teased her. They seemed to know that this little dog had no chance of catching them.

My ponytail flapped against my neck with each stride and my immediate world synced into one rhythm—my breathing, my legs, and the waves—as my feet seemed to float down the beach. I let myself focus completely on my motion.

Until Pip sprinted ahead with a different bark that I was unfamiliar with. She meant business.

A hundred yards or so in front of us, a statue-like figure caught my attention. As I drew closer, the person moved from one pose to another. Yoga on the beach? I was intrigued. Pip wasn't and she was too far ahead of me to catch her before she leaped through the air, hitting the woman hard enough to knock her backwards onto the sand.

I let out a horrified scream as I ran to catch Pip and intervene before she decided to do some real damage.

Scooping the yapping terror into my arms, I held a hand out to help the woman up, my face flaring with embarrassment.

"I'm so sorry," I said. "I don't know what she was thinking. Are you okay?"

The woman refused my hand and stood up quickly, brushing off sand from her legs and arms before she turned an angry gaze on me. "Isn't there a leash law in this town?"

"Not on the beach." Actually, I had no idea if that was true or not, but I said it with great authority and hoped she would believe me.

She harrumphed her displeasure.

I held my hand out again and mustered my most ingratiating smile. "Danielle Mackenzie."

After a pause, the woman gave my hand the briefest shake. "Ava Fontaine. My husband said I'd have the beach to myself in the morning. I never expected to be mowed down by a ten-pound maniac." She moved a couple steps away from the growling menace in my arms and glared at Pip as though she might have a communicable disease.

"Maybe if you let Pip sniff your hand, she'll be okay." I stepped closer to Ava.

One perfectly plucked eyebrow shot up as if I'd just suggested that she eat a bowl of week-old lobster carcasses. "I'm not a dog person."

Along with her perfect tan, her immaculate bleached blonde ponytail and fancy nails, her attitude made me dislike her immediately.

"Well, then," I said, at a loss as to what I could say next to mollify her. She looked like the litigious type. Was she going to tell me she had a whiplash from Pip's enthusiastic lunge?

"Do you live here?" I asked, nodding at a house,

barely visible behind the boulders and sand behind us. That was a neighborly question, but I sure hoped this wasn't Rose's neighbor. They would never get along.

"This?" She flicked her wrist as if I'd pointed to a slum. "Thank goodness, no. This house doesn't even have its own movie theater or spa. No, Marty promised me a waterfront property with every amenity available. It's the only way I'd agree to leave New York City for this backwater town." Her eyes went all glassy for a moment. "I'm trying to endure that rental until we get into our *own* place."

"Oh." How do you respond to that insult? I had a few ideas, like give her a good slap, or let Pip attack her again, but neither of those choices would reflect well on me. Unfortunately. "And where is *your* place?" Hopefully, in another country on the other side of the world.

"Marty, that's my husband, he wants to surprise me, but I told him, 'Marty, hurry it up or I'll be back in our penthouse apartment and you'll be out a lot of money because I won't come back for a second look.'" She leaned closer to me like she was about to reveal something super-secret. I leaned toward her. "He already bought a worthless piece of marsh from a slimy real estate guy. I'm about done with this plan Marty cooked up."

I suddenly had a burning curiosity to find out more about this Marty Fontaine.

He sounded exactly like someone who might want a slimy real estate guy named Ray, dead.

CHAPTER NINE

After my conversation with the doll-like Ava Fontaine, I'd lost interest in jogging. Instead, with Pip tucked securely under my arm so she couldn't cause any more trouble, I headed back the way we'd come. A leisurely pace gave me time to cool off after my encounter with the insulting woman.

With Ava only a small blip in the distance, I set Pip down and let her have her freedom on the beach again. She looked behind us, then at me. She had a proud and satisfied expression, and I was sure she was telling me that she'd scared off an evil woman, protecting me from something dreadful.

I laughed and thanked her for her hard work.

I started jogging back home and my new BFF

followed, lapping at my heels. "Let's see if Rose has cooked up any breakfast yet, Pip," I said. "We need to fuel up for the rest of the day."

As we approached the steps that led up to Rose's home above Blueberry Bay, I was struck by its simplicity tucked among a stand of pine trees, the weathered gray shingles blending in with the natural landscape. This home that had withstood many storms was my safe place. With my grand-mother at the helm and wonderful childhood memories, it stood as a beacon of security.

I sprinted up the steps, hearing Pip right at my heels. The top, opened onto Rose's stone patio over-looking the beach. My three favorite people sat together, two expected and one a surprise—Rose, Lily, and Luke. Okay, I admit, Luke belonged in my circle. If I was honest with myself, he'd never left that special place, even when we'd lost touch with each other. I was surprised, though, to see him there this morning. Rose hadn't mentioned he was joining us.

Luke must have noticed my confused expres-sion. "Rose invited me to swing by for breakfast."

"That's right, I like having you young folks around." Rose said as I plopped in the chair next to her. "How was your jog, Dani?"

Pip, her tongue hanging out and needing a drink, took her spot in the shade under my seat. I took her cue and pushed the dish of water Rose had set out, close to her.

"Interesting," I said, mopping my brow with my towel. I turned to Rose. "Have you met your neighbor, Ava Fontaine? She and her husband, Marty, are renting a house not far from here." With both tea and coffee on the table, I chose my favorite and poured a cup of tea from Rose's flowered teapot.

"Ava and Marty Fontaine." Rose pursed her lips and glanced down the beach as if she expected to see those neighbors. "What does she look like? Tall, thin, probably too much Botox for her own good?"

I shuddered at the memory of Ava's over-manipulated looks. "I guess you know who I'm talking about. She was doing some yoga on the beach. I don't think she's too fond of our," I made air quotes with my fingers, "backwater town."

Rose lowered her head, looking at me over the top of her reading glasses. "She said *that*?"

"And …" I paused for emphasis, "her husband had some dealings with a slimy real estate guy." I looked at Lily. "Her words not mine."

"Maybe she was talking about someone besides Ray." Lily crossed her arms and pouted, as if in his defense. I was reminded of the glow the deceased often took on that seemed to erase some of their defects while alive.

"Maybe," I said, "but I don't think so. She also said Marty bought a worthless piece of land. Didn't you tell me that Ray unloaded something with the promise of a waterfront property?"

"So?" Lily said. I swear, she sounded as if she would take out anyone who had a bad word to say about her late husband.

"Well, Ava said Marty has a super-secret deal in the works. But," I shifted sideways in my chair so I could see everyone straight on, "what if Ray sold him that worthless piece of land and then couldn't deliver on the waterfront property he promised? Maybe Marty wanted to teach Ray a lesson."

Luke, who had been sitting quietly while I spun my tale, came to life. His eyes darkened and his voice took on a bit of a growl when he said, "I think I know this Marty Fontaine guy you're talking about. Ray brought him out to the farm for a look around, thinking Dad was alone and they could pile on the charm and sweet talk him into selling. Only problem was, I was home. I don't think I made any friends when I kicked them off the property and explained exactly what would happen if they returned."

I looked at Luke, confused. "But you don't have waterfront property," I said, trying to understand what was going on with Marty Fontaine. "Ava certainly didn't have expectations of living on a blueberry farm. She needs all her," I threw my hands up in air quotes, "*amenities* like a home theater and spa."

Lily covered her mouth, catching most of the coffee that spurted out. "She told you that? How long were you talking to her? It sounds like you and Ava worked up quite a friendship on the beach."

"Oh yeah," I said, giving her a side eye. "I'll be meeting her tomorrow morning for beach yoga at seven. And then we're going to do each other's nails."

"Really? That doesn't sound like your kind of thing, Dani."

Lily could be so gullible it almost made me feel guilty teasing her. She finally realized that I was being sarcastic, and she rolled her eyes at me.

I drained my tea before it got cold, and then continued. "I almost forgot to tell you guys the best part. Pip here," I reached under my chair and scratched her chin. "Pip attacked Ava."

A chorus of excited *She didn't!* greeted that news from my audience.

"Oh yes she did! She leaped through the air like some sort of ninja fighter and knocked Ava over backwards right into the sand. I'm pretty sure she's got sand in her shorty shorts and she'll be itchy-scratchy all day."

Rose let out a good belly laugh. "Now *that*, I would have liked to see. Pip the ten-pound, terrible terrier versus the beach yoga-lady—tickets only ten dollars, all money donated to the local animal shelter." She crossed her long legs and adjusted her colorful skirt. "Should that be in the next issue of the Blueberry Bay Grapevine?"

We all had a good chuckle at that image. I was sure Ava would *not* see the humor. I wasn't even sure if her face could manage a smile. "I promised Pip some breakfast, which she earned after her brilliant performance. What does everyone want to eat?"

"You're cooking?" Luke asked. "I've always loved your cheesy, pepper omelet." I admit, a warm glow crept up my spine when he smiled at me. But then I saw him lick his lips and figured it was for my omelet, not my company. At this point, I'd take what I could get, so I said, "Okay, everyone. If Rose is stocked up on eggs, I'll make you all omelets. Come on Pip, I'll get your breakfast first."

Luke jumped up from his chair. "I'll help, maybe grate the cheese or chop the peppers or just keep you company?"

Maybe I'd misread his enthusiasm for my cooking. When I slowed to let him catch up to me, I couldn't miss the way his question expressed hope but also allowed me an easy out if I didn't want help … or him keeping me company. "Sure, all of the above," I said.

Rose grabbed Lily's arm before she could join us. "Call us when breakfast is served. We're going to enjoy the view a little longer." Then she sat them both back down in their chairs.

Right, I thought. I could see through her charade of staying outside and letting Luke keep me company. My heart did a little dance—giddy and nervous at the same time.

"It's great to be back on the east coast," Luke said. "I've missed Blueberry Bay."

Was that all he missed? "How's your dad?"

Luke shrugged. "It's been getting harder and harder for him to keep the farm going. I had a tough decision to make but … things happened and coming home turned out to be the best choice. I'm really happy I was around when Ray brought that slime ball, Marty, around. I could tell Dad was starting to give in to his sales pitch and I hate to think what would have happened if I hadn't been there for that visit."

I led the way through Rose's living room into her kitchen. As familiar with her kitchen as if it were my own, I gathered the ingredients I needed— eggs, milk, cheddar cheese, and a red bell pepper. Giving Luke the cheese, pepper, grater, knife, and cutting board, I grinned at him and said, "You volunteered, so get to work."

While I cracked and mixed the eggs with milk and spices, I relaxed and enjoyed Luke's company. "Sorry to hear about your divorce." I guess I was, and I wasn't.

When I didn't hear a response, I turned around to look at Luke. Had I said the wrong thing? He held the cheese suspended above the grater. His face had the pinched expression of someone caught in a very awkward situation.

"Who told you about a divorce?" he asked.

"Rose. Why?" My stomach began to clench. I didn't like where this was going.

He seemed to remember what he was supposed to be doing and got back to grating the cheese. "She must have been talking to my dad. It's not exactly the situation, Dani."

It was my turn to forget what I was doing until the butter in the pan sizzled and smoked. I turned off the burner and moved the pan before I managed to blurt out, "You aren't divorced? You mean it's not final yet?"

Luke set the grater and cheese on the counter. The silence filled my ears with a deafening awkwardness.

He spoke across the room, but not quite at me. "I had to come home to help on the farm, but Jennifer decided to stay in California. I'm sorry if you got the wrong idea about me being home."

I waved my hand like his comment was the silliest thing I'd ever heard. "Don't worry about it, Luke. So…you and Jennifer?" I tried to keep the sob out of my voice.

"Right. Maybe I should leave."

Before I could think of anything to say to stop him, because I wasn't sure I wanted to, he turned and left. It shouldn't have felt so painful. After all, it wasn't the first time he'd yanked out my heart and shredded it like the mound of grated cheese on the counter.

Pip must have sensed something because she

put one little paw on my leg and looked up with big soulful eyes.

"You're right," I said to her with tears streaming down my face. "What do I need him for anyway? I've got you." I picked up my ten-pound bodyguard and hugged her close.

She wiggled and licked my ear.

Without a second thought about what Rose or Lily would think, I walked out of Rose's kitchen before the walls closed in on me. I grabbed the keys to Rose's dark green MG on the way to the garage, hit the garage door opener, and settled Pip on the passenger seat.

"Buckle up, Pip. We're going for a ride."

Pip sat as tall as possible and looked straight ahead, still only barely able to see over the dash. She gave a little woof, which I took to mean *I'm ready, what the heck are you waiting for? Adventure is my middle name.*

I zipped out of the garage without a backward glance, not sure where I was headed, but the MG would get me there and Pip would be by my side.

CHAPTER TEN

I shouldn't have been surprised that I wouldn't get far before my phone chimed. Rose's name popped up on the screen. Should I answer? I had to.

I pulled to the side of the road. "Hello, Rose."

"You left my kitchen a mess. Have you been kidnapped?" she asked. "Is everything okay, Dani? If you don't answer, I'll know someone is holding you at gunpoint, and I'll call AJ to track you down."

I felt bad that I'd worried her. "Yes...no. I needed some air...and distance."

Silence greeted my ears. I sighed, knowing I had to say something. I decided to try the truth. "Listen, Luke isn't divorced, and I kind of made a fool of myself."

I couldn't tell if she made a joke or was serious when she said, "Oh, what did you do? Throw yourself at him?"

"Nothing like that. Pip and I are taking a ride so I can clear my head."

"I know you're taking a ride. My MG is gone. Please be careful and don't scratch it."

I heard Lily shout in the background. "The omelets are almost done, come back and get some breakfast in you before you do something dumb in a fit of hunger. You know you don't make good decisions on an empty stomach, Dani."

Rose's voice came through weary but with her never ending touch of love attached. "She's right, honey. Let's sit down together and make a plan."

I lowered the phone and looked at Pip, her tongue hanging out. "What do *you* think we should do?"

"Dani? Are you talking to Pip?" Rose's muffled voice came through the phone. "Let *me* talk to her."

That sounded so ridiculous I had to laugh. *I* could talk to Pip; she was sitting right next to me, but Rose talking to her through the phone? Why not? I held the phone to Pip's ear and heard Rose say, "You're the sensible one in that car, tell Dani to turn around and come back for breakfast. I've mixed up rice and ground chicken for you, Pip. If Dani hurries, we'll even save something for her."

I jammed the phone between my shoulder and ear while I turned the car around. "She's licking her lips, Rose. I think you swayed her when you said the magic word. *Chicken*." I let the phone drop in my lap and punched end call.

"Traitor," I said to Pip, but deep down I was relieved to know that Lily and Rose had breakfast waiting.

A black BMW raced by me, almost running me off the road into the rocks that acted as the guardrail on this bad corner. I glimpsed a blonde behind the wheel.

"Where are you going in such a dreadful hurry?" I screamed at the fool, but she had passed me.

"Was that your yoga enemy?" I asked Pip. "If it was, she needs more yoga in her life to get rid of that road rage." One more black mark against her, not that she needed any more.

After I parked in the garage, I turned to my companion. "We'll go for a longer drive later, okay?"

Pip's tail waved like a flag on a windy day. She made my heart soar.

"Come on, Princess Pip, breakfast is waiting." She didn't hesitate to jump out and follow me inside. I loved how she trusted me completely. It must be because I rescued her from that terrifying ordeal at the diner. "What happened to Ray?" I asked her.

She didn't answer but I decided there was a fifty/fifty chance that she would point me in the right direction when the time was right.

A pleasing aroma of bacon, eggs, and toast assaulted me—in an exquisite, mouthwatering way —as soon as I stepped inside Sea Breeze. Pip dashed straight to the kitchen.

She was no fool.

Rose had set the table for four in the kitchen nook with a view of the bay. A small bouquet of wild buttercups surrounded by Rose's blueberry plates napkins, and silverware looked like a page from a designer housewares catalog.

Rose had appointed Lily her assistant and she cast a hello over her shoulder as she put the finishing touches on breakfast.

The place settings concerned me. "Is someone else coming?"

I hoped Rose hadn't roped Luke into coming back. I'd face him at some point, but not yet.

Before anyone could answer my question, Pip jumped onto the built-in window seat and burrowed into the cushions as if she'd enjoyed her breakfast here every day of her life. I laughed at her cheekiness. Rose gave me a peck on the cheek by way of welcome back and set a small bowl in front of Pip with the promised rice and chicken, treating her like the honored guest Pip clearly thought she was—breakfast guest number four.

Pip dug into her food without any encouragement, and I realized that she probably hadn't eaten much since the day before. I admired her manners; she didn't inhale the food all at once, nor make a mess. She carefully and methodically cleaned the bowl without one bit of rice spilling on the table.

I, on the other hand, stuffed a piece of bacon in my mouth and was reaching for another piece when Rose slapped my hand. "Go wash up and stop acting like a cavewoman, Dani. You're lucky we made enough for you after the way you ran out of here without so much as a see you later, Rose and Lily."

"Sorry," I said, heading for the sink with a mock hangdog look. Rose put up a pretense of anger at my behavior as a cover for her worry about me. I'd seen that act before. I deserved the pangs of guilt for my thoughtless behavior; I should have known better. I know how she worries. But the fact that they had made enough breakfast for me, spoke to her forgiving nature. That was my beloved Rose.

"Sit down and tell us what happened," Lily said when I finished drying my hands on a towel. She slid a plate with toast, bacon, and an omelet with cheese oozing out the ends in front of me before she sat down across from me with her own plate. Rose sat opposite Pip and the best view from the table.

"Nothing much really happened, I suppose. I was enjoying Luke's company while he grated the cheese. He said how happy he was to be back here. I told him I was sorry to hear about his divorce—which was sort of a lie—and he froze with the cheese in one hand and the grater in the other."

Rose shook her head in disgust. "If Luke isn't divorced, his dad must be losing his mind," she said. "Spencer told me that Luke was divorced, and he moved back here for good."

I drummed my fingers on the table. "Well, he's not divorced, I don't know how long he's planning to stay, and I couldn't have felt like a bigger fool when he corrected me."

"Did you get mad and tell him to leave?" Lily asked. It was a fair question.

"No. I just mumbled something stupid and he left. He must have known how embarrassed I was, or maybe he was embarrassed. I don't know, but I don't think I can ever look him in the eye again."

Rose reached across the table and wrapped her hand around mine. "Don't shut him out. He needs all of us to be his friend now more than ever. There's something else he told me when he found out about the murder weapon."

"My rolling pin? Don't tell me Luke touched it while he was making the blueberry delivery. No one is supposed to touch that rolling pin except me!"

I didn't like the look of concern knitting Rose's brows together when she dropped her bombshell. "He put the rolling pin on top of the invoice to keep it from getting knocked off the counter. He didn't know our system of tacking it to the bulletin board, so he grabbed the first thing he saw to use as a weight."

I dropped my head into my hands. "That means his fingerprints are on the murder weapon. He was in the diner, he touched the murder weapon, and he argued with the victim. Twice if you count the time Ray brought that Marty guy out to Blueberry Acres and Luke told them to get lost."

Rose squeezed my hand. "He's very concerned how it all looks to the police. Unless someone comes forward that saw him at the stop after the Little Dog Diner, he thinks it's only a matter of time before AJ arrests him. That's why we," she gestured around the table, "need to make a plan before AJ thinks he has this murder all wrapped up in a nice neat package with Luke in jail and the key thrown out in the bay."

This was all too upsetting. Not Luke. No matter how battered my heart felt at the news I wouldn't have a chance at getting him back after all, I certainly didn't want him jailed for a crime he didn't commit. But before I could tackle that problem, I picked up my fork and dug into the omelet. "Okay," I said, "But after we eat. Like Lily said, I'm not good on an empty stomach."

Pip had licked her bowl clean, and she was now curled up on the pillows in the window seat. She serenaded us with soft snores that sounded between the clinks of our forks on the plates, and her nose twitched as she dreamed away. Maybe tackling yoga-lady again. Pip seemed to have adjusted to her new routine without any side effects that I could see. A hearty appetite. Check. Sleeping well. Check. And most important, she hadn't wandered off in search of Ray. We were definitely a team now.

I wiped the last bits of omelet up with my toast, washed it all down with orange juice, and leaned back in my chair. "Thank you, Rose, for feeding me. I didn't even know how hungry I was. Now, what's the plan you've been talking about?"

Rose picked up her coffee cup and held it between both hands as if she needed to soak up the warmth. "Lily has an appointment to talk to Frank and Nick Wilde about Ray's funeral. Dani, you're going with her to help with the details."

"But—"

Rose raised her hand and cut me off before I could express how unhelpful I thought I'd be. Especially since other Lemay family members most likely would object to my butting in, judging by their reaction to my entrance at Ray's *fake* funeral. None of the Lemay's had ever held much fondness for me, and I was sure they wouldn't want me around for his real service.

Rose was firm. "No buts, Dani. Lily needs you there for support. Ray's family will try to push her around, and I want you to smile sweetly and tell them to bugger off."

I grinned. "I can do that. And I'll enjoy it, too." Which was exactly why Rose gave me that job.

"Also," she paused to make sure I was paying attention. I was used to that trick of hers. "You'll keep an eye on Ray's family members, on Frank and Nick Wilde, and anyone else who shows up. I'm thinking that the family lawyer will nose around. Ray was the type to cross all his T's and dot his I's. He might have expressed specific details about his last wishes. His lawyer could be running the show."

"What do you think Lily?" I asked. I wasn't sure if all this talk about Ray's funeral was hard for her. After all, she *had* been considering a reconciliation.

"I think I'm ready to stick it to his family for everything I can."

I looked at Rose who had her eyebrows raised to match what mine probably looked like. Sometimes Lily managed to surprise me. "That's perfect, then."

"We need to be at the funeral home in a half hour. And, Pip is coming, too. That will really annoy Ray's mother. She hated it when he adopted her."

I could tell that Lily was already relishing her

new role as the grieving widow with power she never had during her marriage. I chuckled. Where had this side of Lily been hiding? It didn't matter. I was glad she'd finally tapped into it.

"And there's one more thing I need you both to help me with," Rose said. "Normally, I can handle all the articles in the Blueberry Bay Grapevine, but this murder is much bigger news than I'm used to dealing with. I'll need you two to do some interviewing for me."

I rubbed my hands together like I was warming up for all this activity. "That gives us the perfect cover for asking questions without looking like we're doing something we shouldn't be sticking our nose into." I practiced what I thought might be my professional interviewing voice—deeper than normal and a bit stilted. "Hello, I'm working for the Blueberry Bay Grapevine. Where were *you* between ten and twelve on Monday morning?"

"*Perfect.*" Rose smiled her I-mean-business smile with its double hint that she couldn't wait to get to the bottom of this mess.

Pip, perky and refreshed from her power nap, jumped off the pillows. The little eavesdropper must have heard everything we said, and she was ready to get to work, too.

Great. The sooner this murder was solved, the better for everyone. Luke could focus on Blueberry Acres; Lily could figure out her future; Rose could stop hovering over me (maybe); and I could get back into the Little Dog Diner and do what I did best—feed people.

CHAPTER ELEVEN

Lily had managed to bake the blueberry coffee cake while I was off in Rose's MG having my little pity party. She had it packed in a covered container, ready to go, in the time it took me to take a quick shower and change my clothes. My outfit options were limited to a denim skirt paired with a light blue and pink striped blouse, which I decided wouldn't offend anyone when we met with Ray's family to figure out his funeral.

"Take my MG," Rose offered as I slipped my purse over my arm. She reached across the counter and slid the keys toward me. "I know how much you love it, but please, Dani, be careful and don't park near any of those monster SUV's."

I grinned my thanks and hugged my grandmother. She gave me an extra tight squeeze and whispered, "Keep your eyes open, your mouth closed, and your ears tuned into everyone's comments. You don't need to be the show today, just Lily's supportive best friend." She pushed me away to arm's length. "Got it?" She zipped her fingers across her lips for emphasis and added, "Especially, mouth closed."

"Got it, Rose. You can count on me." I wanted so much to please her but the part about keeping my mouth closed might get me into trouble. I'd have to work extra hard on that one.

She narrowed her eyes and glowered at me like she was about to reveal a state secret. "And one more thing. Watch how Pip behaves around anyone you meet today. It wouldn't surprise me one bit if she has leftover anxiety from yesterday's murder. She might be able to clue us into whoever killed Ray."

"Pip?" I suppressed a grin because she was serious. "If we're looking at suspects based on Pip's likes and dislikes, then Ava Fontaine has to be at the top of *that* list. She attacked that woman with a vengeance that made me proud. I don't doubt that Pip would have tried to shake her like a rag doll if I hadn't scooped her up in time."

"Good point," Rose said. "It wouldn't hurt to find out Ava's whereabouts for Monday morning. Renters like the Fontaines might fly under AJ's radar."

Lily tugged on my arm impatiently. "We've got to get going, or I'll be late, Dani. You can follow me."

After another quick hug with Rose to channel her love and strength, Pip and I got in the MG and followed Lily into town. Pip put her front paws on the dashboard, which gave her enough height to see everything and provide support when I took the corners a bit too fast. Keeping up with Lily was no small feat.

"Drat," I muttered to Pip as I searched the full parking lot in front of Two Wilde Funeral Home. Time for Plan B. With the safety of Rose's MG in mind, I drove to the edge of the universe. That's what it seemed like when I found a spot at the far end of the lot away from the pickups and SUVs likely to ding the precious sportscar. I quickly locked up, and Pip and I jogged to catch up with Lily who had zipped into the last vacant spot close to the entrance.

She stood behind her car waiting for us, and I asked, "Nervous, Lil?" when I walked up to her. I fiddled with the collar of her shirt that had gone awry and tucked some blond wisps of hair behind her ear.

She pulled her long braid over her shoulder and bit her lip. "A little. Thanks for coming with me. Do you think Pip will behave herself?"

"I hope not." I nudged Lily, and she laughed. I hoped it helped to calm her a bit. We needed to be on our toes and not miss anything important. "Ready to shake up this meeting?"

After a long inhale and a slow exhale, Lily nodded.

As we headed for the enormous front door, Pip dashed ahead prancing like the little princess she was. "She knows this place, Lil. I bet she came here a lot with Ray while he planned the fake funeral. Was he close to Frank and Nick Wilde? I mean, like real friends or were they just business associates?"

Lily paused before she pulled the door open. "Because of Ray's big ego, he thought everyone adored him. He loved to say that he never met anyone who didn't become a new best friend after five minutes. I suppose that means he really didn't know what it meant to be a friend. He defined friendship as how someone else could be of use to *him*." With her hand still on the door, she added,

"Thinking back, whenever I saw Ray with Frank or Nick, they were always cordial to him, but I don't think they liked him as a *friend*. They had to be nice because Ray owns this building."

"*Owned* the building, Lil. You know what that means?"

"What?"

"*You* own it now. Frank and Nick will be falling all over you to make you think you're their newest best friend. Watch out for those two brothers."

Lily didn't budge from her spot. "I'm not sure I want all the responsibility that fell in my lap because of Ray's death. His family will have their knives sharpened and ready to stab me in the back. Maybe not literally, but I hadn't thought about the business angle and all that comes with it until just now."

Pip scratched on the door. "Someone's ready to go inside. Let's follow Pip's lead and see where it takes us, Lil." I linked my arm through hers, pulled the door open, and we walked inside Two Wilde Funeral Home like we owned it. Well, one of us almost did.

Pip trotted along the dark red carpet past several rooms set up with rows of chairs. At the end of the hallway, she turned straight to the last room.

It had no casket, so I scratched it as a viewing

room. However, the oval mahogany table set up with at least ten chairs was begging for a meeting to take place. A coffeemaker on a cart dripped its liquid caffeine into the glass carafe. Pip jumped onto the chair nearest the windows and made herself comfortable.

I looked at Lily. "Is this where we're meeting?"

Because of the extra cushy carpet, I never heard footsteps approaching, but I certainly felt the hand touch my back, which raised the hair on my neck.

The voice attached to the hand addressed Lily, though, not me. "You're a little early, Lily, but come on in. I see you brought Danielle. And is that Pip sitting in Raymond's seat? Oh, excuse me, where he last sat?"

Lily, to her credit sounded cool, calm, and collected. "Hello, Frank. I brought a blueberry coffee cake to go with your, umm, refreshments." She cast a disapproving eye at the lonely pot of coffee as she handed her offering to Frank. "Where's Nick?" The other half of the Two Wilde Funeral Home owners.

I swear he salivated as he accepted Lily's coffee cake. "Nick will be right along," he said with a slick smile. "Don't worry. Make yourselves comfortable while I pour you both some coffee."

He increased the pressure on my back, and I had no choice but to walk into the conference room. I chose the chair next to Pip and signaled that Lily should sit on the other side of her.

Frank concentrated on fixing a tray with coffee, cream, sugar, and slices of Lily's coffee cake. Perhaps when you work with dead people you don't develop the skill of serving refreshments and talking at the same time. He opened up when he placed the tray on the conference table and indicated we should help ourselves, apparently freeing his mouth for conversation.

He addressed Lily first. "You must be devastated over what happened to Ray. You know, he was working on transferring this building to us. He said it was time to divest and focus more on his marriage."

He gave her a smile that was as fake as a pink plastic flamingo stuck in a snowdrift.

I tried not to gag.

A steaming cup of coffee appeared in front of me, but Frank's attention was on Lily. He was doing a great job trying to soothe her into some kind of trance with his low, deliberate voice.

"What's your offer for the building?" I asked.

His hand jerked, sloshing coffee onto the highly

polished surface of the table. My question threw him off, just like I had hoped it would. I smiled sweetly and grabbed a napkin off the tray to mop up the mess.

"Is that any of your business, Danielle?" Frank gave me a mind-your-manners glare.

I arched one eyebrow and shot back a your-little-act-isn't-working-on-me sneer. "As a matter of fact, Frank," I said, "it is my business because Lily and I are partners."

She kicked my foot under the table. We were partners at the Little Dog Diner, so why couldn't I expand a little to help her out in other parts of her life?

Before anyone had a chance to respond, Pip, who had been eyeing the coffee cake, jumped on the table, slid across the slippery surface, and crashed into the tray spilling coffee onto the dessert and turning everything into a soggy, sticky mess that oozed dangerously close to the edge of the table.

I looked at Frank. His mouth hung open.

"You'd better find some more napkins or a cloth or something before this mess drips on your carpet." I pushed my chair back, trying to be helpful but the damage was done. Frank's face was red with anger.

"I always told Ray to keep that dog out of here," he fumed. "She's nothing but a pest. She knocks the flowers over, nips the customers, and she even piddled on the carpet a few times." He pointed at me. "You and the dog have to leave."

I gave Lily my best injured pout. "It's your building, Lil, what do you want me to do?" I loved playing this good guy–bad guy thing with her even if she didn't know that was the plan.

Lily stood up and brushed the wrinkles out of her dress. "If you're serious about wanting to buy this building, Frank, I suggest you clean up this mess so we can get our meeting under way. Dani and Pip stay with me. That's not negotiable."

I pressed my lips together to keep my laughter inside instead of letting it bubble out in front of Frank. At this point, laughing in his face wouldn't be helpful. I also managed to corral Pip, get her off the table, and minimize cute doggy prints on the rest of the gleaming mahogany surface.

It was the least I could do, but Frank didn't even thank me.

CHAPTER TWELVE

W hen Frank left the conference room, I assumed to get cleaning supplies, Lily and I looked at each other. What started as a few suppressed giggles and snorts quickly turned into full blown uncontrolled laughter. Good thing we let that out, because as Rose always told me, it's not healthy to choke down a laugh for too long.

Pip, free to roam around the room, set off sniffing in every nook and cranny, which made me think that this probably wasn't the first time the carpet had experienced some sort of food malfunction. Her nose was having a field day. So, I got to thinking about the building we were in.

"Lily, did Ray ever mention wanting to sell this building like Frank suggested?" I hoped we had sufficient time to share some basic information before anyone returned.

My question set off a puzzled expression on Lily's face. "He said the Wilde brothers wanted to buy it, but I don't remember him telling me he planned to sell. Do you think I should?"

I darted my head around the door, making a surreptitious glance down the hall to make sure no one was eavesdropping on us. "The coast is still clear," I whispered, but I stayed close to the doorway to keep watch. "Before you make any decisions, you have to find out the details in Ray's will. And then you'll have to talk to your lawyer. It's not something that will happen soon no matter what you decide to do. But you sure can have some fun toying with Frank if you want to. My advice is, keep him dangling on a hook and off balance."

She nodded like she thought that was a sound plan. "Did you notice his nervous habit?"

"Not really. He came across as jittery, like he might be hiding something but not anything that I'd call a habit. What did you see?"

"He kept rubbing his earlobe." Lily's fingers went to her own ear and she fiddled with her earring. "It was like he was used to having an earring to fidget with but there was only an empty hole when he dropped his hand."

I patted the pockets in my skirt. "Darn. I'm not wearing the same skirt I had on for the fake funeral. Remember that sparkly earring I found on Ray when he was still in the casket? I slipped it into my pocket. Maybe it was Frank's."

"Ewww." Lily wrinkled her nose. "You put his earring in your pocket? Are you going to give it back?"

"I don't even know if it's his." I put my finger to my lips. "Shhh. Someone's coming."

Based on Pip's reaction when the intruder entered, this new person wasn't welcome. With the same fury I'd seen on the beach, Pip charged full speed at the invader.

Pip growled, and Ray's sister yelled, "Get that dog out of here." Then she jumped behind me when Pip tried to bite Rhonda's ankle. She sneered, "Too bad whoever killed Ray didn't take care of his dog, too. She's a menace to ankles everywhere."

My mouth dropped open at the sheer contempt in her words. "Only if Pip doesn't like someone," I said. I tried to keep my tone calm but even I could hear my scorn. "And, it makes me wonder why she doesn't like *you*, Rhonda."

I picked up Pip and scratched her belly, which distracted her enough to send her back leg into a twitching frenzy.

"What are *you* even doing here?" Rhonda asked as she moved several paces away from me. She planted her hands on her hips and a sneer on her face. "This is a meeting to plan Ray's funeral. You're not part of the family." She directed an if-looks-could-kill glare at Lily, "*or* a friend."

Like a nervous crab, Frank rushed in with a handful of rags and some kind of spray cleaner. "This will only take a sec and we'll be able to get on with the planning," he said in a singsong voice. The he noticed Rhonda and flashed her a smile before he cleaned up the mess.

"Frank!" Rhonda's voice came out whiny and grating. "What is Danielle Mackenzie and Ray's horrid ankle-biting dog doing here?"

Frank gathered up his soiled rags and I saw some kind of silent communication pass between him and Rhonda. I sent Lily my own silent look letting her know something funny was going on between those two. She returned a slight nod, so I knew we were on the same page.

I settled myself in Pip's chair, thinking it was the

seat with the most power since it had been Ray's seat. Pip was happy to share with me.

Rhonda scowled her dissatisfaction but made no objection to my seating choice. *She* chose a spot as far away from Pip and me as possible. I patted Pip's head letting her know she was still an excellent judge of character.

"To answer your question, Rhonda," I said, "Pip and I are here at Lily's request. As Ray's widow, she has every right to have me at her side. Is that a problem for you?" I smiled, even though it hurt me to do it.

"Of course not," she said, as her head moved up and down. If that wasn't a contradictory answer, I didn't know what was but at least I knew exactly where she stood—not liking me one bit.

"Who are we still waiting for?" Lily directed her question to Frank.

"Nick should be here shortly. Are your parents coming, Rhonda?"

She sniffled and used an embroidered handkerchief to dab at the corners of her eyes. "It's too painful for them and," sniff, sniff, "as Ray's devoted sister, they asked that I represent their wishes here today."

Rhonda almost sounded sincere, but when

Frank patted her hand and they shared another look, I couldn't help but wonder what show the two of them were putting on for us. It could just be a mutual attraction between two lonely people, *or* it could be a mutual cooperation between two people up to no good.

Then I saw the nervous habit that Lily mentioned earlier as Frank fiddled with his earlobe.

"Sorry I'm late." We all turned as Frank's younger brother, Nick, rushed in. "I was consoling a grieving family. So sad." He pulled out a chair between Rhonda and Lily and sat down.

Pip tensed briefly at this latest addition, but I stroked her back, and she curled up on my lap with a long, contented sigh. Was this an endorsement of Nick? Too soon to tell, but I'd keep my eye on Pip in case she took a dislike to him. In the meantime, I gave the latecomer my full attention as he started the meeting.

"Ray's attorney, Mr. Fulton, called and said he couldn't make it today but would reschedule at a time that works for the family," Nick said. "So, is everyone here now?"

Lily nodded and stood up. Her hands trembled slightly, but as she began to talk, her voice strengthened. "Thank you all for coming." She looked at each person at the table. Frank reached for his earlobe, Rhonda looked away instead of meeting Lily's eyes, Nick shuffled through papers he'd brought to the meeting, I nodded and smiled at my best friend, and Pip snored.

"I would like to have Ray buried in the white casket he used yesterday for his fake funeral."

Rhonda gasped.

I covered my mouth and coughed to cover a laugh that would have been inappropriate.

"And I want white lilies surrounding the casket."

Rhonda pushed away from the table, sending her chair crashing onto the thick carpet behind her. Frank rushed to right it. "I can't believe this. You," Rhonda pointed her long, red fingernail at Lily, "are making a mockery out of Ray's murder."

Much to Lily's credit, she looked appropriately stunned when she replied. "Don't you think, Rhonda, that Ray chose the white casket and white lilies because that's what he liked? Do you have any information to show me that he'd prefer something different for his final send off?"

"Of course not. Who plans their own funeral?" Her hand shot up to cover her mouth, but it was too late to shove those words back in.

I'd had all the absurdity I could tolerate for one

day. I felt my eyebrows shoot up and my mouth failed to follow Rose's advice. "Someone with an ego bigger than Blueberry Bay? Someone who was known to deal less than ethically with his real estate transactions? And this, in my opinion, is the worst side of Ray Lemay," I looked at everyone in the room. "Ray Lemay is someone who tried to manipulate his wife by putting on an extravagant *fake* funeral." My voice rose with the last statement as my fury increased. "Should I go on, Rhonda?"

Frank stood next to her, wringing his hands and his face contorted as if he had a fishbone stuck in his throat.

I had to assume that this was not the norm for most funeral planning meetings. Too bad because I was enjoying it so much more than I had expected to.

Nick picked up his stack of papers, tapping them on the table until they were in a nice, neat rectangle. "I have all of Ray's plans for his...*event* yesterday right here with me. Lily, should we, Two Wilde Funeral Home, proceed according to these guidelines?"

Lily's braid was coming undone, which seemed to signal her growing impatience with the proceedings. "Yes, please, Nick," she said, a little abruptly.

"That's exactly what I'd like to do. I think Ray knew best what he would have wanted so there's no sense in changing *anything*." Lily tilted her head and squinted at Rhonda. "You're missing one of your earrings."

Rhonda felt her earlobe and then looked at Frank. His fingers nervously touched his own earlobe.

I tucked Pip under my arm and got out of my chair to check for myself. "Let me see what your earring looks like, Rhonda." Her dark hair was pulled back into a tight bun, exposing one brilliant diamond star shaped stud in one ear and an empty hole in her other earlobe. "I'm not sure if the earring I found matches *exactly* and I don't have it with me…but I'll be sure to check."

She huffed at me and said, "I don't know what you're talking about since I didn't *lose* an earring. My ear is infected, so I took it out." She finished her sorry explanation by shooting me a dirty glare.

Frank took her elbow. "I'll walk you out."

Nick gave me a questioning look. "That was interesting. Frank asked me recently if I'd seen *his* earring. He was kind of upset about losing it, said it had sentimental value." Then Nick shrugged like he found the whole problem ridiculous. "I guess if the one you found is his, he'd probably like it back." Returning the conversation to business, he asked Lily, "We'll have the funeral on Sunday?"

"Yes, Nick. Sunday at three in the afternoon."

He made a note on one of his papers. "Very good. You're in excellent hands with Two Wilde Funeral Home. I'll take care of everything, Lily, but call if you have any questions or changes. Otherwise, I'll see you on Sunday." As quickly as he'd come into the room, Nick left.

I wiped my sweaty forehead with my arm. "You did great, Lil. Let's get out of here before Rhonda comes back for our heads, or at least mine. I don't think she likes me very much."

With Pip tucked securely under one arm, I held the other one out for Lily. We walked out with our heads high, and shoulders back, which was our preferred way to enter or exit this place.

CHAPTER THIRTEEN

"Where to now?" Lily asked as we left Two Wilde Funeral Home.

"I'm going to my apartment to pack up some clothes. Rose insists that I stay at her place until this murder is solved."

Lily reached her car first. The MG, still parked in a galaxy far, far away, looked like it managed to escape any damage. Pip found a grassy strip at the edge of the lot and sniffed around while we talked.

"Do you think we'll be able to get into the diner?" Lily asked as she pointed her key fob to unlock her car.

I shrugged my lack of insight. "I'll be surprised if the police are done this quickly, but maybe they can give us a time frame. Are you coming with me to my apartment?"

"I guess so," she said, my normally upbeat friend sounding like she had the weight of the world on her shoulders. "I'm feeling a bit lost and I don't know what else to do with myself."

"Oh, Lil." My heart ached for her. "It will work out. Don't expect to tackle everything all at once. One thing at a time and you'll be back in a routine before you know it. I'll follow you to the diner."

Lily climbed into her car, and I walked to the MG. Poor Lily. She had been ready to strike out on her own and live without Ray when she served him with the divorce papers, but he still would have been around. Now, all of his affairs, for better or worse, were in her lap.

"Come on, Pip. Jump in to your spot as my little co-pilot."

Pip eagerly settled on the passenger seat and looked at me with what I assumed meant, hurry up and let's get going. She sure was a bossy little thing when I imagined what was going on in her mind.

When we arrived at the Little Dog Diner, the area swarmed with investigators. I suppose my concern should have been figuring out who killed Ray, but first things first. With yellow crime tape all over the place shutting down the diner, I worried how we would make up these days of lost income.

I pulled into the driveway next to the Blueberry Bay Grapevine and parked behind Rose's Cadillac. Pip scooted across my seat, following me out on the driver side instead of waiting for me to open her door. Ha, bossy *and* impatient.

Entering the Blueberry Bay Grapevine office, I heard Rose hard at work pecking away on her forty-year-old typewriter. She had a computer, too, but she preferred to type her first draft the old-fashioned way. She insisted it made her focus better.

The click-clacking stopped when I walked in. She looked up at me over her reading glasses. "Just in time."

"For what?"

She pulled the paper out of the typewriter and held it toward me. "You can retype my first draft of the fake funeral article while I get started on the murder article."

I took the paper and sat at her other desk and teased her as I made myself comfortable. "Rose, did you actually get information, or did you just make something up?"

To her credit, Rose was diligent about every word she printed.

"I'll have you know," she said, twirling her reading glasses in her hand as she swiveled her chair in my direction, "I interviewed Detective AJ Crenshaw and he shared a few details about the murder. For example, did you know that they found a diamond earring near Ray's body? He needed to know if it belonged to you, me, or Lily. I never saw it before, and he said he'd need to talk to both of you about it."

I threw the paper on the desk. "Be right back," I said over my shoulder as I scooted out the door.

"Dani!" Rose called but I didn't stop. I needed to find that earring from yesterday morning. If it matched what AJ found, well, it would mean something.

I almost mowed Lily down as she hurried into the office. "Where are you off to in such a hurry?" she called.

"Be right back," I answered over my shoulder. "Rose is inside. You can start typing her article for her," I said before dashing up the stairs to my apartment.

I flung open my apartment door expecting this to be a quick in and out errand. But then I almost let loose some salty sailor talk when instead of quickly racing for my closet to search the pocket of my dress, my feet got caught in all of my running shorts and tank tops strewn on the floor, the remains of the tornado that had swept through my place. Instead of spewing four letter words when I realized someone had broken into my apartment, my blood pressure skyrocketed at the disaster left behind.

Stepping over every article of clothing I owned, along with pillows, papers, and countless other movable object, I was in a state of shock as I searched for my little black dress. This was no time to lose my focus when finding that earring had just become my number one priority. Providing the burglar hadn't found it first!

"Danielle? I need to talk to—"

I turned around, surprised to see Detective Crenshaw standing in my doorway, his mouth hanging open as he surveyed what must have looked like a case for hoarders international. "Detective?" I mumbled.

"What happened here?" He stepped inside and closed my door. "Do you need a recommendation for a house cleaning service?"

I couldn't tell if he was serious or sarcastic, but I hastily explained the break-in. "I stayed with Rose last night. By the look of this mess, I'd say someone broke in and trashed my apartment."

"Do you have the family jewels hidden in a coffee can somewhere?"

He could see the sum total of my possessions on the floor. Jewels? Really, he was going there? I rolled my eyes at him.

He stepped over my jogging shorts and said, "I mean why would someone break in to your place?"

After discovering I'd been targeted by some thug, I was in no mood for banter. I said, "Well, you're the Detective, so maybe you can figure that mystery out."

At that, AJ took me seriously. "What I mean, Danielle, do you think this mess could be connected to the murder? Was someone looking for something that you can think of?"

Hmmmm, I thought. Maybe. That possibility had been on my mind. I moved some of the scattered clothes around with the toe of my shoe, hoping to find my little black dress with the earring still in the pocket. My mood plummeted by the second.

"I don't own anything of value." I swung my arm around to indicate my measly collection of treasures. "You can see for yourself—used furniture, old pots and pans, and an assortment of clothes. Unless I see someone walking around town wearing some of my old clothes, I'm not sure I'll even miss anything."

My pulse pounded when I flipped a pillow with my foot, uncovering my dress. Now what? Wait for AJ to leave or tell him about the earring? I picked up the dress.

"Did you find something?" He stepped closer. I should have known that his detective skills would kick in.

"Maybe." I patted the pockets. Nothing. I slipped my hand into one—empty. Then the other. That dang earring had to be hiding in there somewhere. Who would have known to check these pockets? "Ah ha!"

AJ peered over my shoulder.

I held my hand out to show him the sparkly earring. "I found this on Ray's chest when he was in the casket at his fake funeral." I looked at AJ. "Do you think it could be a clue?"

He pulled out a plastic bag and tipped my hand so the earring slid inside. "You found it *before* Ray was murdered and I found a similar looking diamond earring in the diner that might be its mate. I wanted to ask you and Lily if it belonged to either of you."

"Not mine. I don't own any diamond anything. And, I think that earring *you* found?" I paused for added emphasis. "Was dropped in the diner by the killer." I let *that* sink in.

"That's one possibility."

Well, I heard something interesting at Two Wilde Funeral Home when Lily and I were there to plan Ray's funeral. His *actual* funeral."

AJ waited silently for me to continue.

I cleared my throat. "Listen, I don't want to point my finger at someone who may have nothing to do with Ray's murder."

"I understand, Danielle, but you never know what might be an important bit of information. What did you hear?"

I paused. Did I really want to get more deeply involved with this case? Why couldn't I just play dumb, back out, and let AJ and his team do their thing? Why did I have to butt my nose into it? The answer came flying at me like a bee after honey. Because I was onto something and if I didn't pursue it, my best friend Lily could pay the price. So, I plunged ahead with my theory, letting the chips, or earrings, land where they may.

"Frank Wilde has a pierced ear," I began, "but

he wasn't wearing an earring when I saw him. His brother told me he lost it and is hoping to get it back because it has sentimental value."

AJ shrugged, clearly not convinced it was a meaningful clue. "Frank could have dropped it anywhere."

"I know," I said, a little frustrated he didn't get my point. "But this is even more interesting. Rhonda Lemay was at the funeral home for the meeting, too. She was only wearing one earring, because, she said," I threw up air quotes to show my skepticism, "her other ear was infected. But she could have been lying about that. I looked and it didn't seem red or irritated. Anyway, I'm not a hundred percent positive, but that earring," I pointed to the one in the evidence bag, "looks an awful lot like the one she was still wearing."

AJ held up the see-through bag and looked at the earring again. "That makes three earrings—one you found, one I found, and one Rhonda was wearing. Don't earrings usually come in pairs?"

"Of course, they do, but it doesn't mean someone can't wear only one. Right?"

"I'm not exactly an expert on earring etiquette so I'll take your word for it." He tucked the bag in his pocket "You're suggesting that Frank or Rhonda lost an earring in the diner?"

"I'm suggesting that's something to look into."

AJ didn't say anything, but it sure looked like he was filing that bit of information away. As he headed for the door he said, "Don't clean up in here yet. I'll send a team in to dust for prints and look for clues. By the way, was the door locked?"

"Not when I came in just now, so I guess I forgot to lock it. When I left yesterday, I thought I'd be in the diner for only a short time. I hadn't planned to leave overnight, and I guess I forgot to go back and lock up."

"Okay. We'll be able to tell if anyone forced their way inside."

A shiver went through me at the thought of someone breaking into my space. It was creepy, but at least I hadn't been there to see it happen. Or worse. I could replace stuff, but I shuddered at the thought of possible injuries if I'd walked in on the crime. Suddenly, I needed to get out of there. "Can I take some clothes with me now?"

AJ's voice had softened. Maybe he'd realized the danger I was in. "Take what you absolutely need, lock the door, and give me the key when you go back downstairs. You'll be staying with your grandmother?"

"Yeah," I said, relieved in more ways than one at the prospect of hanging out with Rose. "Until the murder is solved. She insisted."

"Good," he said, giving me a look I couldn't puzzle out. "I'm not sure you'd be safe here by yourself, and I don't want to worry about you."

I was stunned. Detective Crenshaw and I had never been, should I say, bosom buddies. Sure, it was his job to protect the people in Misty Harbor, but to tell me he was worried about me? I stared up at him—his neatly trimmed dirty blond hair, bluish gray eyes, and a lean muscular body. He was no longer the kid who used to pull my hair when he sat behind me in math class. Far from the boy I remembered, I was seeing the new and maybe improved AJ Crenshaw for the first time.

"Are you okay, Dani? I need to get back to the diner."

"Yeah, yeah." I flicked my wrist, shooing him out the door. "I'll just grab a few things and be out of here."

He paused in the doorway. "I'm sorry we have to keep the diner closed until at least tomorrow. You'll have a lot of cleaning up to do and you might not be able to open up for business for a while. Whoever trashed your place destroyed just about everything that wasn't attached to the floor. If you need help with the cleanup, let me know. I'm sure I could round up some volunteers to lug stuff to a dumpster."

I gave him a blank smile, still shocked at his kindness.

What had changed in the last twenty-four hours?

CHAPTER FOURTEEN

When I entered the Blueberry Bay Grapevine office, after giving my apartment key to AJ, both Lily and Rose stopped typing and gave me a once over—definitely annoyed. Pip, still curled up on the sweater bed I'd made for her, raised her head and wagged her tail before she settled back into her comfy nest. At least one member of this group made me feel welcome.

"The way you rushed out of here, I had to check to see if the diner was on fire," Rose said in her not so subtle style, letting me know I'd better tell her what the heck was going on. She leaned back in her desk chair with her arms crossed. "Well?"

Before addressing Rose's question, I turned to

my friend. "Lil, remember that earring I found on Ray at his fake funeral?"

She made a big shake of her head to let me know she knew what I meant.

Rose hitched up one eyebrow. "You found an earring?" The disapproval in her voice let me know I'd better get to my story and fast. "And you didn't think you should share that tidbit with me after I told *you* about AJ finding an earring in the diner?" She didn't even try to hide her irritation, but her curiosity won out. "Is that what you rushed out to get?"

I opened her small fridge and helped myself to a cold bottle of green tea with ginger and guzzled about half before my parched throat recovered. "Yes. As soon as you told me that detail, I remembered how I'd tucked the earring into the pocket of my black dress."

"Did you find it?" Lily asked. "Let me see it. I remember exactly what Rhonda's earring looked like—a mini star shape set in either white gold or platinum."

Rose whipped her head around to stare at Lily. "What does Rhonda have to do with all this?"

I sat down next to Pip and scratched under her ear. She sighed and lifted her head so I could reach her favorite spot. "I'll start at the beginning. When Lily and I were standing at Ray's casket, I saw something sparkly on his chest. Obviously, it didn't belong there, so I scooped it up, stuck it in my pocket, and forgot about it until you mentioned that AJ found an earring." I twirled my finger in a circle. "Fast forward to our meeting this morning at Two Wilde Funeral Home." I drank the rest of my tea giving Lily a chance to jump in because the next part was her story.

"I noticed how Frank had a nervous habit of rubbing his earlobe," she said, "you know, like some people do when they're turning an earring?" Lily demonstrated just in case we were too dense to understand the concept. "Anyway, his ear is pierced but he wasn't wearing an earring."

Rose shrugged. "Maybe he decided it fell out of fashion. *I've* never been a fan of men wearing earrings."

"Maybe," Lily continued. "But according to Nick, he *is* upset about losing it because it has sentimental value." She paused to get our reaction, but I gave her the move it along sign. "So," she said, "Maybe it has sentimental value because of who gave it to him. Anyway, when Rhonda got all huffy and was about to leave, I noticed she was missing one of *her* earrings and the one she was wearing was…guess."

"A diamond stud in the shape of a star." Rose tapped her fingers on her desk. "Did you find the earring you stuck in your dress pocket, Dani? Does it match?"

"I found it."

Lily charged across the office, almost falling into my lap. "What are you waiting for? Let's see it." She held her hand out.

"I don't have it."

Both Rose and Lily shouted "What?" at the same time. "You got us all worked up about a potential clue that could solve the murder and you don't have it?"

"You won't believe this but when I went up to my apartment, someone had broken in and trashed the whole place."

Lily's eyes bugged out bigger than an owl's. "I told you I thought I was in danger, but I never thought *you* would be." Her words came out in an exhale of air, barely audible. "Were they looking for the earring?"

"I don't know what they were looking for or if they found anything useful but," I grinned. "They didn't find the earring."

"So, where is it, Dani?" she asked.

"AJ came up right after I got into my apartment. After he got over the shock of the mess, he asked me if *I* had lost a diamond earring. You both know that's about the most ridiculous question anyone could ask since I don't own anything of value. Anyway, I found my black dress under a pillow, dug the earring out of the pocket, and showed it to AJ. He took it as evidence."

"Wow!" Lily hugged me. "I'm so sorry."

"What are you sorry about? I didn't want that earring. And now I'll have to have that dress dry cleaned to get the earring ick out if I ever plan to wear it again."

Her face drooped, and I could see this latest episode added to her worries. She confirmed that when she said, "I'm not sorry about the earring, Dani. I'm sorry I dragged you into my drama with Ray and put you in danger, too."

Rose took Lily by the shoulders and eased her back to her seat. "Why do you think you're in danger, Lily?" I could tell Rose was in full comforting grandmother mode.

Lily set her elbows on the desk and propped her chin in her upturned hands. "This whole reconciliation thing with Ray?" Lily sighed so deeply I wasn't sure she could keep going, but she said, "I think he wanted someone to think he was really dead. I think that's what the whole fake funeral was about. He told me he had been getting a lot of mysterious phone calls at work and on his private number. The caller would hang up after a bit of silence. Not only that, cars would speed by his house in the middle of the night. He hadn't been sleeping well."

Whoa. This was new news. "But Lily, you told me the whole fake funeral thing was to prove to his family that you really did love him and wanted to reconcile."

"That's true and then we were going to sneak out and disappear until he figured out who was stalking him and why."

"But you ran out of Two Wilde Funeral Home with me, so the plan fell apart," I said.

By now Lily's hands were trembling and her voice shook with emotion. "It's all my fault that Ray was murdered. I got cold feet and messed up his plan. If he hadn't come to the Little Dog Diner to meet me, he'd still be alive." She blinked, but I could still see her eyes glistening with tears.

I put my arm around her shoulders as she struggled to hold her tears back. "It's not your fault, Lil. Ray didn't have to run after you. He could have left by himself and stayed safe if he was really in danger."

She looked up at me, as if she thought some kind of answer was written on my face. I wished I could take away her pain and grief. "What if he was coming to warn me? What if he had more information about the stalker?"

"All the what if's and second-guessing are pointless, Lily," Rose said, staring out the front window of her office. "Ray made his own choices." She turned to Lily. "All you can do—we can do—is get to the bottom of what happened and move on. Let's find out from AJ if the earrings match, which still won't prove anything but it's a thread to follow."

Rose looked at me. "I'm still confused about all this earring business. Would there be any logical reason for Frank and Rhonda to have matching earrings?"

I paced across the office. "Something strange was going on between those two this morning. I'd put money on the fact that they're in a relationship or something like that. Frank was hovering over Rhonda like she was a piece of delicate china, and they kept sharing meaningful glances. Maybe Rhonda gave Frank the earring that he lost."

"So, what?" Rose said, still staring into the

distance. "You think that one of them lost an earring during the fake funeral and the other one was lost in the diner? Along with the earring that Rhonda is wearing, that makes three. There should be a fourth one floating around somewhere." She draped her hobo bag over her shoulder. "Let's see if AJ will share any more information."

With three strides Rose was at the door, pulling it open, and scowling at Lily and me. "Are you coming or not?"

I tucked Pip under one arm and pulled Lily out of her chair with the other. When Rose latched onto something, she was like a dog with a bone and nothing would get in her way. She didn't like to wait for anyone, so we got our feet moving before she left us too far in her dust.

I kept a tight hold on Pip to keep her out of the way with no chance for her to irritate AJ again. Rose had him cornered outside the door of the Little Dog Diner by the time we caught up with her.

"The earrings, AJ? A match or not?" I heard Rose ask with her don't you dare try to lie to me tone.

Lily, Pip, and I were behind her now, like we had her back.

"Yes, Rose. The earring that Dani found and

the one from the diner match. But until I do more investigation, I'm not going to jump to any conclusion, and I don't want you to either. And this information stays out of your article for now. Understand?"

We all nodded. It didn't mean I couldn't try to find out where Rhonda and Frank went after Lily and I stormed out of Two Wilde Funeral Home Monday morning.

Someone lost an earring in the diner and it wasn't me, Lily, Rose, or Pip.

CHAPTER FIFTEEN

While Rose wrapped up her conversation with AJ, I spotted Ava Fontaine standing on the sidewalk. A medium tall, dark-haired man stood next to her glowering to let anyone who was interested know he wasn't pleased with something or other. Since he had wrapped his hand possessively around Ava's waist, I had to assume he was her husband, Marty.

Not wanting to miss this opportunity to get information, I raised my hand and waved as if I'd just seen a long-lost friend. "Yoo-hoo. Ava!"

Her partner, dressed in madras shorts, white golf shirt, boat shoes without socks, and reflective sun glasses, leaned close to her ear and must have whispered something because her face took on a pinched expression. He was probably wondering who the heck Ava's new friend was. I marched in their direction anyway, determined to corner them like a fly in a spider web. Pip squirmed, forcing me to let her down before she leaped from my arms, risking a broken bone. I pretended I'd forgotten Pip's dislike of the crazy yoga-lady.

She darted straight for Ava's ankles. The woman shrieked like a two-year-old and jumped behind her partner. To his credit, he crouched down to intercept Pip, who fell for this friendly gesture.

Traitor, I thought. I decided I'd given Pip too much credit in the character analysis department.

"Ava, I'm so glad to bump into you again. Remember me? We met on the beach this morning?"

I knew there was no chance in a million that she forgot meeting Pip and me, but, whatever, I could play the game to get what I wanted. "And this must be your handsome husband, Marty." I held my hand out after he stood up with Pip in his arms happily licking his chin.

Ava gave Pip a look that could kill. "That's disgusting, Marty. Put that dog down. She almost killed me this morning."

Marty was fighting off Pip's attention with head bobs and a big smile. "Oh, come on, Ava. This little thing couldn't hurt a flea." Marty quickly shook my hand then positioned Pip so they were eye to eye and said in the sing-song way people talk to animals, "You're too cute for your own good. Ready to go back to your mom?"

Pip wagged enthusiastically, always a sucker for a kind word. I wasn't convinced she'd gauged this guy correctly, though.

"We were looking for a place to eat. Why is the diner closed?" Marty asked.

Ava broke in, speaking to her husband as though he were a disobedient child. "I *told* you, Marty. That real estate guy was *murdered*."

"Here?"

Ava cast her eyes so high I thought they might get stuck under her brows. Was this a new yoga exercise? "You *never* listen to me. I *told* you someone killed him at the Little Dog Diner." She pointed to my pride and joy. "*That* place, which doesn't look like it serves edible food anyway. Let's *go*, Marty."

Okay … I was ready to take my gloves off when she insulted the Little Dog Diner food—mine and Lily's food—food that the locals all loved. "Excuse me?" I clenched my fists and considered letting Pip loose on this horrible woman.

Lily, now at my side, must have sensed something was about to happen. "Did you know," she said, "that the Little Dog Diner is the hottest eating spot in all of the Blueberry Bay area?"

"Well, after the murder, it will probably be the most *avoided* eating spot in the Blueberry Bay area," Ava mimicked Lily's tone. "Who will want to sit anywhere where there was *blood* and *gore* on the floor? It should be torn down, in my opinion. We are probably witnessing the *death* of the Little Dog Diner." She looked at Marty. "Maybe you'll be able to start that upscale restaurant after all when this property goes on the market."

My jaw practically hit the sidewalk. Marty wanted to replace the diner with a fancy schmancy establishment? I looked at Lily and whispered. "Another lie Ray fed you? Didn't he say *he* wanted to open a fancy place for *you* to manage?"

"He wasn't lying, Dani. They probably stole his idea."

I hadn't considered that.

Ava, oblivious to everything but herself, continued whining. "I'm *hungry*, Marty."

"Why don't we go back to the house and eat

there? We can enjoy the view of the bay. Wouldn't that be nice, honey?" He rubbed her back affectionately.

Ava pulled her head into her shoulders like she was pretending to be a turtle. "I don't want to *make* something. You *promised* to *buy* me lunch."

I actually felt a tad sorry for henpecked Marty. I seriously wondered what this relationship had in it for him besides a thin, overly made-up trophy wife to parade in public.

"You know," she continued, "I wouldn't mind investing in a restaurant if we can't get the waterfront property."

Ava had her own money? Interesting. "Marty?" I asked. "How long have you two been in town?"

"A couple of weeks, I guess. Why?"

"I suppose you've looked at quite a few properties, right?" I shifted Pip to my other arm.

"Enough. For instance, I've had my eye on these two buildings that the diner is nestled between. I do think that a new restaurant with a chef from New York would bring tourists flocking into town."

Rose took that moment to join us. "Guess what?" I asked her.

She cocked one eye, which meant she probably didn't want to hear what I was about to say.

I said it anyway. "Rose, these are your new neighbors, Ava and Marty Fontaine. They had their hearts set on eating at the Little Dog Diner and since it's still closed, I thought it would be nice to invite them to your house; have some lunch; get to know them better. Okay?"

"We couldn't impose," Marty said.

"Shut up." Ava jabbed him in the side. "Don't be rude."

Rose looked like she was ready to send me to my room with no lunch, but instead she smiled. "How nice. I can't think of anything I'd rather do. Luke will be joining us, too, Dani."

She just proved that two could play at this game, and she was much better at it than I was. I suspected this lunch would be filled with land mines along with our sandwiches and iced tea.

"We'll head home and then walk over," Ava said. "You're the house next to ours?"

"That's right…Sea Breeze," Rose answered. "Just follow the steps up to my patio."

After Ava and Marty left, Rose turned on me. "What are you thinking, Dani? I heard them say they want to buy my property and the diner. I'm not sure I can gag any food down if they're sitting at my table. Plus, he wants to buy Blueberry Acres. How will Luke manage to be civil?"

"Listen, I agree, but we have to find out where they were yesterday morning. Ava shoots off her mouth like a drunken sailor. I'm thinking if we serve her some wine, and get her relaxed, we might get some useful information. With Luke there too, the tension might draw Marty out."

Lily had been quiet up to now, but she tossed her braid over her shoulder and said, "Dani's right, Rose. They have a motive to kill Ray. I think they stole his idea about the upscale restaurant. With Ray out of the way, it would be full steam ahead. I can just imagine Ava parading around as the owner dressed in a tight red dress and loads of jewelry while her New York friends oohed and aahed over her brilliant new place. It makes me want to throw up."

"And you know you aren't going to sell, so let's butter them up and find out as much as we can," I said, hoping Rose would see this as a winning strategy. "Lily and I will make lobster salad if AJ will let me get food out of the diner's freezer. Do you think he'll let me do that?"

Rose nodded. "I've noticed how he's been

looking at you, Dani. Is something going on between you two?"

I felt my cheeks burn with embarrassment. "Nothing that I know about, but if it helps me get inside, I might flutter my eyelashes a few times. What do you think?" I wiggled my shoulders and made my best flirty face.

"Don't play with fire or you might get burned," Rose answered.

I wasn't sure what she was thinking with that statement as Pip and I approached AJ, but in order to keep my request professional, I didn't lay on any of my special charm. "Would you consider letting me get some food from the freezer?"

"Sure. I'll escort you inside." He put his hand on my back and whisked me into the diner like I was some sort of royalty instead of a part owner. "What do you need?"

"Some lobster for our lunch and maybe a blue-berry pie for dessert." We walked around all the flour and mess still on the floor. I tried not to think about the disaster, but even with my focus on the freezer, I couldn't ignore the crunching under my feet or the conversation of investigators doing their job.

"Sounds delicious. We haven't had time to stop for lunch today."

Was he angling for an invitation or trying to distract me?

We stopped in front of the walk-in freezer. "Okay, Dani," he said. "Get what you need, but I'll have to check everything before it leaves the diner."

I handed Pip to AJ. "Here, I'll need both hands." I ignored his shocked expression and complained, "You make me feel like I'm stealing my own stuff, AJ."

I completed my list, held up each item to show him, and stacked them on top of each other—a blueberry pie, lobster meat, and rolls. "That's it," I said. "No, wait, I'm adding a bag of frozen blueberries to have on hand until I can get back in here."

"Okay. Enjoy your lunch," AJ escorted me past the crime scene and out the door where I enjoyed a deep cleansing breath of fresh air.

I had successfully hidden an envelope taped to the top of the blueberry pie under the other items. This secret at the bottom of my stack of food made me feel like I *did* actually sneak contraband out of the diner.

AJ put Pip down. "I think Ray would be happy

that you've taken charge of his beloved little dog." He paused, then put his hand on my shoulder. "You know, Dani, I've been thinking about Ray a lot lately. He and I were drifting apart. I don't think he liked me telling him he was headed for trouble with, what I considered to be, unsavory characters. I told you this before, but it needs repeating—be careful, you *and* Lily."

My heart pounded from this warning and the mystery of the message in Luke's handwriting taped to the frozen blueberry pie in my arms.

CHAPTER SIXTEEN

I casually walked to the Blueberry Bay Grapevine driveway, feeling Detective AJ Crenshaw's eyes on my back the whole time. I couldn't figure out what, if anything, his new friendliness meant, but I planned to chalk it up to him doing his job as a dedicated employee of Misty Harbor. No sense in reading anything more into it, especially since I had no interest in AJ, except as a friend now that he wasn't behaving like a silly teenage boy any more.

With the food balanced on one arm, I opened the passenger door for Pip. By now my little companion knew the routine and happily settled into her spot as my co-pilot.

I put everything I took from the diner's freezer

on the floor in front of the passenger seat. Fortunately, Rose's Cadillac was already gone so, I had time to read the letter from Luke away from her prying eyes.

I tore the envelope off the frozen pie and stared at my name written in Luke's distinctive left-handed style. It brought back memories of letters he wrote to me when he first left for college, before things fizzled out between us. A deep sigh escaped my lips as I slid my fingernail under the envelope flap. I slipped out the single sheet of paper that was neatly folded in thirds.

Dani,

I'm back to help my father on the farm. Unfortunately, I didn't have the pleasure of bumping into you today when I delivered the blueberries, but our paths are bound to cross. Looking forward to seeing my old friend!

Luke

He hadn't planned to blindside me with a surprise visit after all. I wasn't sure what to make of the note, except I shouldn't overthink it. We were both surprised when Rose invited him into the Blueberry Bay Grapevine office. I decided to give him a second chance after the awkward misunderstanding when we found ourselves together in

Rose's kitchen earlier. Why not enjoy a renewed friendship while he was here?

Why not indeed? I could think of one big reason, which had to do with my fragile heart, but I ignored that in favor of spending time with Luke. We both could use a trustworthy friend, right?

"Ready, Pip?" I turned the key and backed out. AJ waved, sending a chill through me. What did he know about Ray's wheeling and dealing to make him give me *two* warnings to be careful?

"I wish you could tell me something about Ava and Marty," I said to Pip. "You must have been with Ray when he met with them since he took you everywhere. Did they argue? Did one of them threaten Ray?"

Pip looked at me and wagged her tail. Apparently, she liked it when I talked to her, but she wasn't spilling any secrets.

Lily's car was parked in front of Rose's garage, so I left the MG outside. I balanced the food in my arms and led Pip through the front door, following the soft murmur of voices into the kitchen.

Lily had a glass pitcher of what I assumed was her special blend of cranberry juice, red wine, seltzer, and fruit slices—perfectly refreshing for a warm, early summer afternoon and a get-to-know-the-neighbor drink. Rose had filled a tray with silverware, napkins, and plates. Now, I guess it was up to me to finish preparing lunch for our guests.

"Did AJ give you any trouble about taking food from the diner?" Lily asked as I unpacked my ingredients next to the sink.

"No. He only needed to inspect what I was taking away from the crime scene in case it was evidence. Thankfully, whoever trashed the diner hadn't touched the freezer. All the prepared food and frozen ingredients should be salvageable. The rest of the place? A jumbled mess. I'm afraid everything not nailed down might be ruined."

"I've been thinking," Rose said. "Maybe it's time for an upgrade to the Little Dog Diner. It's closed now anyway. Perfect timing. Let's talk to Luke about redesigning the interior."

"What?" I gasped. "Why ask Luke?"

"Ask me what?"

I turned around just as Luke arrived. Before I could catch his eye, he picked up Pip and gave her a cuddle. The dog loved him if her wiggly body and quick kisses were an indication of affection.

I leaned against the counter with my arms crossed. "Ask you about redesigning the diner. Rose thinks this would be a good time for it. What do you think?"

He grinned at me and then Rose. "I think I'll be happy to help with whatever you three want." His smile traveled up to the corners of his eyes, making little creases that spread his version of sunshine even wider. "I don't have a lot of free time, but I could squeeze some renovations in."

"That's settled then," Rose said, cutting off any further discussion. She was like that. What she wanted, she got. I couldn't really argue since she owned the diner building and if she wanted to stick money into it, great. But why hire Luke?

"What about your part time police job?" I asked.

Pip squirmed out of Luke's arms and padded around the floor sniffing for scraps. Luke's eyes followed her for a few moments, then admitted, "Yeah, that's not going to happen."

I must have looked surprised because he said, "AJ's got me on the suspect list, remember? You know…means, motive, and opportunity. It really boils down to the fact that I was in the wrong place at the wrong time. He's having trouble checking my alibi."

Before any of us could commiserate, we turned

toward the voices coming in from the bay side of Rose's home. "Must be the guests. I'd better get going with lunch," I said.

"Guests?" Luke leaned forward to glance through the window overlooking the patio.

Rose explained in a low chuckle, "Dani decided to invite the horrible neighbors for lunch—Ava and Marty Fontaine. You've met them, Luke." Rose picked up her tray and prepared to greet her neighbors. "If you can stomach sitting with them, come on out and join us."

"We'll be out as soon as we finish setting up lunch, Rose," I said as she disappeared onto the patio.

Luke's face darkened at the mention of the Fontaines, which didn't surprise me.

"I don't know," Luke said. "I told you about my tantrum when Ray brought Marty to the farm. Maybe I should leave."

"Wait," I said. "I'm not a fan of them either, but I want to find out where they were when Ray was murdered. According to Ava, Marty has big plans for a lot of property in town, and Ray might have conned them with a worthless chunk of land. That's a motive, right, Lily?"

Lily turned from the salad she was tossing. "Uh-huh. Luke *should* stay. Pretend to reconsider about selling the farm and see where it leads. Ava's an open book, but Marty is more reserved. We have to get him to open up."

Luke tilted his head. "You think Marty murdered Ray?"

"We think it's a possibility that AJ might be overlooking," I said. "Ray apparently had a big plan for an upscale restaurant in town and now Marty is bragging about that same thing. Maybe he wanted Ray out of the way, so he didn't have competition for the property *he* wants—the diner, Rose's building, and possibly the real estate office that Lily now owns."

"I didn't think about that," Lily said. "Marty probably expects that I'll want to unload it. He knows those three buildings make up a prime location in town and he'll try to buy them. If that's all true, Marty is the sleaziest guy I've run into, and we have to stop him."

"Are you in, Luke?" Rose surprised us by popping back into the kitchen to check on lunch. She'd been eavesdropping on our conversation.

"I'm in but only if I get the remodeling job at the diner," Luke answered, giving her a wink. "I want that challenge, and I already have lots of ideas swirling around in my head."

"You drive a hard bargain, Mr. Sinclair, and I love it." Rose said. Satisfied we had everything under control, she looped her arm through Luke's and headed to the patio. "Come on. We'll leave these two to finish making lunch."

Pip trotted after them to check out the guests, too.

"Want to know what I think, Lil?" I said after they'd gone.

"Not usually."

I ignored her dig. "I think Rose is motivated by Ray's idea of an upscale restaurant in town. She's not going *that* route, but I think that's where this remodeling idea came from."

"It's about time. That diner hasn't seen any upgrades since I've been alive."

"True." I wondered what ideas Luke had swirling in his head because I had some of my own. We'd have to work together on this project, which made a smile grow on my face.

Lily tapped the frozen lobster on the counter. "Were you planning to use this today?"

"It was my plan, but I guess my defrosting timing was off. Any other ideas?"

Lily opened Rose's pantry. "There's canned tuna fish, and I'm sure she has cheese, too. How about we whip up tuna melts with," she looked around the kitchen, "tomato slices? How does that sound? Should we check if it's okay with everyone?"

"Are you kidding?" I quickly opened three cans of tuna. "They get what they get, and they don't get upset."

"Ha! I'll bet you a buck that Ava has something to say about it, and I don't mean that in a, thank you-this-looks-delicious, way either." She hitched her hip to one side, tossed her head back, and flexed her wrist like it was a dead fish. "Tuna? That's so common. With cheese? I'm allergic to cheese. I'll just have carrot sticks, please."

I doubled over laughing at Lily's exaggerated accent. "I may as well give you a dollar now because you've nailed her snooty attitude."

Lily filled up a cookie sheet with bread and slid it under the broiler to toast one side. When that was done, I added the tuna fish mixture, cheddar cheese, and tomato slices. "At least they're colorful." I slid the tray back under the broiler waiting for the bread to crisp and the cheese to melt.

"Is it hard seeing Luke again?" Lily asked while I had my back to her.

Good question, and I wasn't really sure how to answer it. I was absolutely shocked when I saw him walk into the Blueberry Bay Grapevine office, and my embarrassment went off the charts when I asked him about his divorce that didn't exist. Now, though, I was looking forward to chatting with him.

"Yes and no," I told Lily. "I'm over the surprise of seeing him, so I hope we can become friends again."

Lily said, "Rose told me she thought she'd really screwed up when she brought him into the office, surprising both of you out of the blue like that. And, she believed his dad when he told her that Luke and Jennifer were divorced. When you disappeared this morning, I had to do some major reassuring to ease her worry."

"I was upset, angry, and embarrassed all wrapped up in an emotional meltdown," I said, cringing at the memory. I took the cookie sheet out. Eight perfectly bronzed tuna melts sizzled on the pan.

"I'm lucky that Pip is a good listener," I said reaching for my spatula, "And she doesn't give advice." I transferred the tuna melts to a platter, snipped some fresh basil over the tops, and looked to Lily for an opinion. "What do you think?"

She gave them a thumbs up. "As good as they'd get at the diner, only don't tell Ava that or she'll be worried about food poisoning."

We shared a laugh as we carried the platter and Lily's salad to Rose's patio table. The big umbrella provided plenty of shade from the afternoon sun and the breeze coming off the bay was as refreshing as a gentle fan.

Everyone had a glass of Lily's wine cooler. Based on the level in the pitcher, she might need to make more.

"I hope everyone likes tuna melts," I said cheerfully as I set the platter on the table. I didn't dare look at Lily or we both might double over in a fit of giggles.

Ava slipped the biggest one onto her plate. "My favorite. How did you know?"

Neither of us saw that coming, and I almost choked on my snort. Lily poked my back and slipped something into my back pocket—a dollar I assumed.

Luke patted the chair next to him and nodded toward me. "Pip saved your spot."

Sure enough, she was sitting in the shade of my chair. She knew where she belonged. Plus, it was out of sight of Ava!

"This looks delicious, Dani," Rose said as she helped herself. "Ava and Marty have been telling us about all their sightseeing adventures around town."

I took my seat, trying to keep my voice light and breezy with our guests. "Been having fun? What have you liked best so far?"

I filled my glass, thinking I'd need several refills to get through this lunch.

"Well," Ava said after she dabbed the corners of her mouth with a napkin. "Yesterday morning we decided to focus on downtown. I discovered the best craft shop with stunning, locally made items. Everything was so reasonably priced compared to New York City. I have to admit, I went a little crazy on my shopping spree." She glanced at her husband. "Marty was bored with it all, of course. He wandered around outside until I finished. Shopping isn't his thing."

I peeked at Rose; she had a satisfied grin on her face.

Me? Well, I had to down a glass of wine cooler. Goosebumps popped up on my arms as an awful realization hit me. There was only one way to analyze Ava's tidbit of information. I was sure that Rose and I were both thinking the same thing – the location of the craft shop, Creative Designs, was directly across from the diner.

How convenient for someone to follow Ray into the diner, whack him over the head, and leave—all in a matter of minutes.

CHAPTER SEVENTEEN

L unch on Rose's patio with her new neighbors was a bigger success than I ever would have expected. Even Luke seemed relaxed and ready to dig for information from Ava and Marty.

Of course, the revelation that they'd been right across the street from the diner when Ray was murdered made us all a little bit giddy. The question remained—had either of them lost that earring in the diner? Ava had more piercings along the outside of her ears than I thought was possible, but I wouldn't know if one was missing. Besides, she'd been in the store shopping. Marty didn't have any ear piercings, which Rose would approve of, but it made it unlikely that he lost the earring.

When the conversation moved to Blueberry Acres, Luke's chair bucked a little and scratched along the patio stones like he'd been jabbed with a hot poker. His profile said it all—clenched jaw and eyes on Marty like a predator about to pounce. He gripped his chair until his knuckles were as white as Rose's linen napkins. I thought he might just rise up and bolt out of there he seemed so disgusted with Marty all of a sudden. But he stayed put, at the ready.

"You know, Luke," Marty said, "even if you don't want to sell, I could give you some ideas to keep that amazing property profitable. I mean I'd love to buy your dad's farm, but I can see that it provides an important product for this area. Great branding with all the tie-ins to blueberries."

Luke furrowed his brow at me. His grip relaxed as he leaned toward Marty. "I'm trying to add events to bring in more people and their dollars. What are *your* ideas?"

"Well, originally, I thought it would be the perfect spot for top-end condos for anyone wanting to escape the city to this lovely town on the bay. The problem with that idea is the influx of people would ruin the town. Right? I'd be killing the main attraction."

We all nodded like sheep. Maybe this guy wasn't so bad after all.

"Here's the thing," he continued with his elbows on the table and his eyes fired up with excitement. "Instead of condos, you convert the farmhouse into a bed and breakfast. Right? With a complete inside and out remodeling, you'd be booked solid. I mean *months* ahead. I'm talking, bedroom suites, a game room, a modern kitchen with an adjacent dining area for your guests and room for the locals, too, if you want. Outside, you'd have to have gardens … walkways, flowers, shrubs…maybe a pool and tennis courts…I'm just thinking out loud here. You wouldn't have to do everything I've suggested but make a plan so you could expand in the future to meet your guests' needs. You could have a shuttle bus to the beach or make bikes available for the exercise minded guests. Honestly…the sky is the limit."

Marty picked up his wine cooler and drained the glass in one long drink. Ava helped herself to a second tuna melt. She already looked bored to death with the talk centered on something besides her. The rest of us? Silent. I know *I* was stunned at Marty's idea. Stunned *and* impressed. It was an awesome plan, in my opinion. Luke could keep his blueberry fields but expand in this new direction. Perfect.

Except, with his wife on the west coast, he probably wasn't planning to stay in the Blueberry Bay area forever. The plan wasn't something he could easily manage from three thousand miles away.

"It's a lot to think about," was Luke's reply as he sat back in his chair. If disappointment had weight, I heard a ton of regret buried in his tone.

Ava had her hand out, studying her nails. She'd only taken one nibble from the second tuna melt. Maybe she planned to wrap it in Rose's napkin and save it for later. "Marty? Isn't it time for that meeting with Rhonda Lemay? I like her much better than her brother, Ray. You know, I'm not sure anyone will be missing *him*."

Lily's face hardened.

Before she had a chance to hurl any threats in Ava's direction, Rose took control of the conversation. "Ava, you haven't been in town for long, have you?"

"Long enough to know who I like and who doesn't deserve my respect. Right Marty? You never liked Ray either, did you?"

"And why is that, Ava?" Rose filled Ava's glass with the last of the wine cooler from the pitcher.

"I've known the Lemay family for generations. They are an important family in the Blueberry Bay area."

"I suppose you might be blinded by that history, Rose, but I have a talent for reading people. Ray Lemay showed his phoniness right from the get-go." She sipped the cold drink. "This is delightful."

"Takes one to know one," I mumbled under my breath. I caught Luke's smirk from the corner of my eye. "And yet you did business with him, Ava, and were hoping he'd find more prime real estate for you and Marty."

She waved her hand as if she were shooing a pesky greenhead fly away. "Sometimes business trumps values, but now we have Rhonda working for us on our restaurant plans."

Lily slowly rose to her feet, keeping her hands flat on the table, unable to contain herself any longer. "I hate to burst your bubble, *Ava*, but *I'm* in charge of Bayside Real Estate now. I'm sorry to tell you, but it won't be business as usual anymore. As a matter of fact, I'm taking over all of Ray's deals." She held her hand out. "Lily Lemay, Ray's widow. I guess I should have introduced myself properly before lunch started."

I had never felt more pride for my friend than

right then when she stared at Ava, and with quiet finesse, put that insult of a woman in her place.

"Well …" Ava drained her wine cooler, "we'll see what *Rhonda* has to say about *that*. *She* said *she* was now the acting president of Bayside Real Estate. That's who I want to work with."

Lily smiled sweetly, but I knew it was forced because her eyes seethed with a dark blue anger. While her focus remained squarely on Ava, I held my breath, eagerly anticipating what would happen next. Lily had found her stride, strength, and supremacy in the Bayside Real Estate hierarchy.

Lily sat down and lifted one eyebrow revealing her skepticism of Ava's comments. "Is that so? How interesting. I always knew Rhonda disliked me with a passion. And the jealousy she harbored for her brother could be seen by some," she tapped the table with her fingernails, a sound like a doom and gloom intro for a bad horror film, "as a motive for murder. I'll be sure to share this information with Detective AJ Crenshaw."

I was close enough to Ava to hear her sharp intake of breath. "Oh, well," she said with a nervous giggle, "our conversation with Rhonda was all just a friendly chat." She looked to her husband for some backup and then back at Lily. "I'm sure you know all those details better than I do and we," she placed her trembling hand on Marty's, "would love to work with *you*, Lily."

This whole exchange left me with more questions than answers. The first one that popped up was if Lily was taking over the Bayside Real Estate business, who was going to be the short order cook when the Little Dog Diner reopened? That thought pretty much pushed everything else out of my brain for the moment. I couldn't do it all by myself. Was I supposed to put an apron on Pip and teach her how to serve customers? I wished that were an option.

But I didn't have time to dwell on my problems. Lily hadn't finished showing everyone there was a new sheriff in town. "The first order of business," she said directly to Ava, "before you're planning gets ahead of you, is to let you know that the three buildings you have your eyes on: the Blueberry Bay Grapevine, the Little Dog Diner, *and* the Bayside Real Estate building are *not for sale*. *None* of them. Today or in the future. So, get your prime location for an upscale restaurant idea right out of your brain. Are we clear?"

Ava nodded and actually looked a bit contrite. On the other hand, Marty, who had been a silent observer through all this, threw his napkin on the table as if he were issuing a warning.

"Anything is for sale if the price is right. That's what Ray understood, and I think you'll have a battle on your hands if you plan to back out of the deal I made with your husband. I *will* have my upscale restaurant with or without your help, and the Little Dog Diner will be swallowed whole when I open for business."

He stood and yanked Ava's arm. "Let's go. I've lost my appetite for dessert."

Pip growled. Her input was too little, too late, as far as I was concerned, but I patted her to let her know her opinion was appreciated.

"What have I done now?" Lily asked. She looked around the table at the three of us still with her.

"Exactly what you should have done, dear," Rose said with a gentle pat on Lily's hand. "I've known bullies like Marty Fontaine my whole life and do you know what they hate more than anything?"

Lily shook her head.

"Someone who questions their ability to carry through on a plan."

It would be an uphill battle for Lily but with

Rose and me by her side, we'd run those two out of town with their tails between their legs. Or, if they killed Ray, tell AJ to throw the key away after he locked them up.

"You'd better find out what Ray was up to as soon as possible," Luke advised Lily. "You'll need the upper hand with someone like Marty Fontaine.

Luke was right of course, and we kept reminding her of that as the four of us—Rose, Lily, Luke, and me—enjoyed huge slices of blueberry pie with a healthy dose of ice cream before we cleaned up the dishes.

Then we thanked Rose for lunch and after saying goodbye to Luke, headed straight to Ray's office at Bayside Real Estate. It was beyond time for Lily to understand what Ray had his fingers mixed up in. We planned to search through all of his papers, emails, texts, and anything else that could be lurking in what had been his domain.

Lily was taking control of the reins.

Rhonda would be furious.

CHAPTER EIGHTEEN

M ain Street, running through Misty Harbor was quiet this afternoon compared to the past couple of days. After Ray's murder and the closing of the Little Dog Diner, our little town looked like a film shoot for a cop show with all the uniforms and crime scene tape. Now, it was filled with tourists spending their dollars everywhere except the Little Dog Diner. It broke my heart to think about all the meals that weren't being served and the pies that weren't being baked.

But right next door, at Bayside Real Estate, it was a different story. Several cars filled the parking spots out front.

"It looks like Rhonda hasn't wasted any time

getting her greedy self over here," Lily said. "What trouble is *she* stirring up?"

It was more of a statement than a question, and I could tell she didn't expect a reply. We both knew the answer: plenty.

"And isn't that Frank Wilde's car?" I asked Lily as Pip's wagging tail led us to the front door.

Lily grinned at me. "What do you want to bet that we'll catch the both of them up to no good?"

"A dollar." I fished the dollar I won from Lily out of my pocket and held it up to show her. "Here, I'll just give it back to you now."

Before Lily had a chance to pull the door open, Nick Wilde barreled through, almost knocking us off the step. He managed to get a hold of both of us and kept us from landing in a heap. "Sorry. I guess I wasn't paying attention like I should have been. Are you okay?"

I pushed my hair out of my face. "Yeah, fine, Nick. What's up?"

He rolled the cuff of his sleeve up, probably embarrassed about the blue stain that I noticed. Nick lived alone and evidently couldn't be bothered worrying about laundry. "Frank and I were hoping to talk to Lily about the status of our building, but Rhonda barged in and said *she* was in charge." He shook his head with a hint of disgust. "I wish she'd mind her own business."

Lily placed her hand on Nick's arm. "Listen, Nick, this isn't a good time to talk about any real estate deals. I've got a lot to sort through and get myself up to speed with this business. Everything is on hold for now."

"I understand. Call when you're ready for an offer." He smiled and hustled down the steps. "Oh, I almost forgot, but did you do anything about that earring you said you found? Frank is still checking every drawer and pocket he can think of. He even crawled around on his hands and knees in his office but with no luck."

"Actually, I turned it over to Detective Crenshaw, so if Frank thinks that it's his, he can go to the police station and identify it."

"Such a big deal over that little bit of vanity," Nick muttered before continuing to his car.

"I wonder if Frank *will* ask AJ about the earring," Lily said as we walked up the steps.

"If he bashed Ray over the head, it's the last thing he'll be doing," We reached the front entrance of the converted old home turned into a realty office, and I held my hand out. "You first."

Lily pulled the door open with the new power

she'd recently discovered. I leaned close. "How are you feeling, Lil?"

"Ready for a battle that I should have fought long before now. I never even realized how Ray drained my confidence. Now I'm asking myself why I *ever* considered a reconciliation. I can't wait to find out what he's been hiding in his papers. I suspect it will be eye opening."

I certainly wasn't the person to disagree with her conclusion.

On the heels, er, paws of Pip, acting as if she owned the place, we marched through the entryway and reception area, and headed for what had been Ray's office in the back. No one said a word as we passed by a couple of agents at their desks pretending to be hard at work.

Voices drifted into the hallway as we got closer to Ray's office. Lily turned her head, her pinched eyebrows letting me know she was as confused as I was about who belonged to the voices.

I pulled her up short, picked up Pip, and put my finger to my lips. With a nod toward the wall, I inched us off to one side, staying out of sight but within earshot. Better to know what we were walking into than having an unpleasant surprise, I told myself as a way to justify our eavesdropping.

We heard a woman say, "Where did he put those contracts?"

I stared at Lily, finally recognizing Rhonda's hushed but clear voice. We crept closer to the wall in an effort to hear more of what she had to say. When Rhonda said next, "I searched her friend's place, too," I wanted to swoop in with guns blazing, but Lily held me back and we just continued snooping.

". . . just in case Ray's sneaky wife found them," she continued, "and needed a hiding spot. That was a waste of time. All Dani has is old beat up furniture and second hand clothes. If it wasn't for her grandmother, she'd probably be living on the street."

Lily squeezed my arm, stopping me from charging inside and doing something I would surely regret. At least I had a name I could give AJ for the lawbreaker who trashed my apartment.

We held our breath waiting for what came next.

"Are you sure all the signatures were in place?" Frank asked. "How did Ray ever convince Lily to sign off on my building?"

Lily's hand flew to her mouth, but a tiny squeak still escaped. I held my breath.

Rhonda laughed. "Don't worry about *that*,

Frank. As long as you have the tickets for our honeymoon all set, the rest of our plan will fall into place perfectly."

"I don't know." The doubt in Frank's voice came into the hallway loud and clear.

"Oh, Frank." Then silence.

Lily and I took great care to peek around the corner of the partially opened door, wondering what had captured their attention.

My hand flew to my mouth at the sight of Rhonda wrapped around Frank in an embrace that left no room for the imagination. Lily pushed me out of the way, which made the door swing into a coat stand. The coat stand tipped and crashed onto a chair. Pip jumped from my arms straight into this scene.

No point trying to hide from that ruckus. I barged right in.

Frank's eyes popped open, seeing us before Rhonda had a chance to turn around. He shuffled away from her and picked up a big set of keys from the desk. "I'd better get back to work, Rhondy. Nick will be wondering what held me up here."

I made an educated guess that Frank wasn't the mastermind behind whatever was going on between these two. He exited the office quicker than a seagull snatching a sandwich.

"*Rhondy*?" Lily, with her don't-mess-with-me voice, ambled around Rhonda and plopped into Ray's chair behind his ultra-modern, glass-topped desk. She propped her crossed ankles on the desk and settled back in the chair. "What contracts are you looking for? Maybe I can help you find them."

Rhonda's head swiveled between Lily and me before she made a decision. She pulled a chair close to the desk and made herself comfortable, too.

Pip and I stayed near the door as Lily's backup, ready to enjoy this confrontation. I had my money on Lily.

"Well, Lily, I was trying to finish up some loose ends." Rhonda shrugged and flicked her wrist dismissively. "Just trying to be helpful, take some of the burden off your shoulders."

"That's very thoughtful. And Frank? He was helping you?"

"As a matter of fact," Rhonda leaned forward so she could put her hands on the desk, "the contract I was looking for has to do with the Two Wilde Funeral Home building. Maybe you didn't know this," she said with condescension dripping from her words, "Ray just finished negotiations to sell the building to Frank. It's nothing you need to worry about, though, everything is all set."

"Right, Frank did mention that to me." Lily removed her feet from the desk and propped her elbows there instead. She tapped the tips of her fingers against each other somewhat impatiently. "As I recall, though, Ray wasn't interested in selling. What changed?"

Lily's strategy of laying out a web for Rhonda to get stuck in had me clenching my hands with frustration. I wanted her to charge ahead for the kill.

Rhonda, sounding full of confidence, answered, "Oh, you know Ray. One minute he was going in one direction and the next minute, he changed course a hundred and eighty degrees."

They both shared a laugh at Ray's expense.

"So, I'll just keep poking around until I find the contract," Rhonda said.

"Actually," Lily crossed her arms over her chest, "*my* plan is to put a hold on all business until I've had a chance to review each and every document before moving forward. You know, since this is *my* responsibility now, I have an obligation to make sure everything is in order."

"But—"

"No but's about it, Rhonda. I'm sure Frank will understand." Lily made a big deal of using a key on her key chain to unlock a document size drawer in the desk.

I wished I could see Rhonda's face as she jerked forward to look over the top of the desk. "What's in *there*?"

Lily slid out a stack of manila folders, taking her time to straighten them before piling them neatly in front of her. The snail's pace was killing me, and I could only assume that Rhonda was ready to explode.

"Well, how about we take a peek."

Lily flipped through the folders, reading off the names connected with each transaction. She slipped one folder to the back of the pile without reading the name. "Nothing here involving Two Wilde Funeral Home."

Rhonda stood up. "What are your plans for Bayside Real Estate, Lily? I'm trying to be patient with you, but until today you never had even the tiniest interest in this business. Ray did *everything* here, and he promised *I* could have a more senior position, even be a *partner* soon. You can't possibly think you know enough to run this real estate business." She sat back in the chair and crossed her arms

A twitch next to Lily's eye was the only indication that Rhonda had overstepped her boundaries. I casually sauntered around so that I had an unobstructed view of Rhonda and Lily's faces. I needed to know what was coming. Since I'd run out of patience, I decided to give things a nudge.

"Rhondy." I liked the sound of Frank's pet name for Ray's sister. "How did you feel about Ray and Lily getting back together? I'm guessing that might have been a teeny tiny problem for your plans to climb the ladder here?"

I could feel the temperature shoot up in the room. "What is this?" she snapped in a heated retort. "You're ganging up on me now?" Rhonda glared at me. Hate dripped from her tone thicker than molasses in winter.

"As a matter of fact," she snarled, "it was Ray's opinion that Lily *couldn't* run this business." The corners of her lips got stuck between a grimace and a smile. "I have to wonder, Lily, with Ray dead now, *you* get everything instead of only half if you waited for the divorce to be final. What do I get? A big fat *nothing.*"

Was she really asking for sympathy with the pouty mouth she gave us?

I was only one step away from her now. "Rhondy, I hope you aren't suggesting that Lily murdered her own husband, because I'd take that as a threat to my best friend."

Rhonda smirked at me. "The whole reconciliation was a scam just like that funeral. Ray only wanted to protect himself and his assets from her greedy divorce threat. Lily was on board with the whole scheme. You didn't know that did you, Dani? Your best friend was scheming behind your back."

I scoffed in her face. "Nice try to divide and conquer but my friendship with Lily is as deep as Blueberry Bay. Are you seriously trying to paint Lily as Ray's killer?" I threw my hands in the air and laughed in her face. "Lily has an alibi. You didn't know *that* did you, Rhondy? And while we're on the subject of alibis, where were *you* after Ray's funeral fell apart?" I reached out and pushed her hair behind her ear. "And where is your missing diamond star-shaped earring? Did you lose it in the Little Dog Diner?"

Rhonda slapped my hand away. "My ear was infected, so I took the other earring out. Not that it's any of *your* business. Where was I after the funeral fell apart? That's none of your business, either." She walked out with an air of victory.

Maybe she didn't want to admit it, but Rhondy hadn't won a darn thing.

CHAPTER NINETEEN

Lily sagged into Ray's old chair. "I'm exhausted from that interaction with Rhonda. How will I ever manage this whole real estate business, Dani?

"Don't worry about that now. I'm more interested in what's going on between," I made quotations with my fingers, "*Rhondy,* and Frank. What shenanigans are they up to anyway?"

Lily perked up a little. "Don't forget what she said about searching your apartment. She was looking for contracts."

"Exactly and I noticed you snuck one of the folders to the back of the pile." I reached across the desk and slid the bottom folder out. "May I?" I asked before I opened it.

"By all means," she said.

The label said Lemay holdings. I flipped it open and scanned through the various properties. The last entry caught my attention. "This is interesting, Lil. This is a contract to sell Two Wilde Funeral Home to Frank Wilde. Did you lie to me about that? Were you hoping to hide this from me?"

Lily jerked upright in her chair and it bounced against the desk. "No!" she said adamantly. "What are you talking about? I didn't lie. I didn't want Rhonda to get her grubby hands on it until I had a chance to check it out first."

She grabbed the papers from me and flipped through to the signature page. Her face turned to a pasty gray and she showed it to me. "That's not my signature. I never signed this, Dani. Someone forged my signature."

"Ray?"

"Or Rhonda. That would be my guess, but I'm not sure. Here, take a closer look." Lily handed the paper to me.

"If I didn't know better, I'd think this was your signature."

"Right? But I've never seen this document before. Ray never talked to me about it and," she stabbed her finger on her name, "I did *not* sign this."

"Okay. Okay." I held my hands up and paced around the office taking in the details, hoping to find a clue of some sort. I stopped in front of a small gallery of photos on a bookshelf. "When was this taken?" I handed her a framed photo.

Her face softened as she looked at the image. "On our honeymoon when I still thought Ray was the sweetest, nicest guy I'd ever met. We had a great time."

I also noted two enlarged photos of Pip on the wall but decided not to bring that to Lily's attention. It wasn't Pip's fault that Ray gave his precious dog a bigger platform than his wife. They were nice photos.

"What do you think of this idea, Lil?" While I'd meandered around the large office, my mind put some pieces in order. "Ray signed your name on the contract. He told you he wanted to reconcile, probably so he didn't have to hand over half of his net worth to you."

Lily's mouth opened but I put my finger up to stop her comments.

"This is just a theory, Lil. He put on that elaborate funeral and promised you a trip because he said he was in danger."

Lily cocked her head like I'd zoned out for the past twenty-four hours. "Well yeah. Have you forgotten? He must have been in danger. Someone killed him, remember?"

Rather than get into an eye-rolling contest with her, and giving a snarky, *of-course-I-know-do-you-think-I'm-an-idiot* retort, I reminded myself her husband had just been murdered. He might have been a creep and a crook, but he was her crook. So, I dialed it back and said soothingly, "Right, but he didn't know he would be killed. I think he wanted to get you out of town so the deal could be finished. Then you'd never know what he'd done. Did you know you'd have to sign off on the property?"

Poor Lily's shoulder's slumped under the weight of all this. "To be honest," she said sadly, "Ray probably could have convinced me that my name wasn't even on the deed."

She hung her head. "Rhonda was right. Ray did do everything in the business, but that's because he didn't want me involved. Now I can see why. He knew I'd never agree to some of the deals he made."

"Oh, Lil." I put my arms around my dearest

friend in all the world and hugged her close to me. Her pain was my pain. "You okay?"

She sniffed and her head nodded against my shoulder. "Thanks, Dani. I'm mad at myself for letting Ray manipulate me. If he wasn't already dead, I'd wring his neck."

That made me laugh and I had to wag my finger at her. "Don't stand on Main Street and shout that threat to high heaven, Lil. There are plenty of folks that might take it the wrong way."

"I'm not stupid." I felt her body sag a little bit; my little joke seemed to have hit a nerve. "You know what the worst part of all this is?"

I had an idea but just in case I was wrong, I shook my head. "What?"

"You were right about Ray. Thank you for not rubbing it in."

What could I say? I hugged her again, glad I had the sense to show some restraint when it came to Lily's relationship with Ray. I finally understood that sometimes it's best to sit back and let the other person figure stuff out for themselves. I wasn't saying it was *easy* to keep my thoughts to myself; I was reminding myself that sometimes it was the smart thing to do.

"Enough of this pity party," Lily said as she let

go of me and returned to Ray's desk. "I'm going to go through all of Ray's papers with a fine-toothed comb and organize everything, so I finally know what was going on with this business."

"Good plan," I said.

"Are you going to talk to Detective Crenshaw about Rhonda trashing your apartment?"

I gave that serious consideration but came up with an alternate plan. "First I want to talk to Luke. He studied criminal justice so he should have good advice for me. At this point, if I wait a little bit, will it make a difference? All I have for evidence is a conversation we overheard."

The edges of Lily's mouth twitched. She saw right through my explanation. "I'm sure Luke will love to help you," was all she said, but I was positive she knew I was using it as an excuse to visit him. "But before you go, let's take a look at the Blueberry Acre folder. After what we discovered about the funeral home, we shouldn't take anything for granted."

"Good idea. Where is it?"

Lily shuffled through the folders until she found it. "One thing about Ray was that he was meticulous about writing everything down. If he had some shady deal planned, the details will be in here."

The file was fairly thick, and I examined each page carefully. I didn't think it was a bad idea to overthink things or be overly suspicious even though Marty had already sounded like he'd given up on buying the farm. But then, I almost missed the most important paper in the folder.

"Look at this, Lil." My stomach churned with fear.

"Did you find something?" She snatched the paper out of my hands and from the speed with which she absorbed the information, I knew Lily was perfectly capable of running Ray's business. Heck, any business.

She looked up at me, her face knotted in concern. "Blueberry Acres owes a hundred thousand dollars to the town in back property taxes? The farm goes into foreclosure if that money isn't paid by," she looked at the page for confirmation and then back at me. "Today," she announced in disbelief. "Do you think Luke knows about this? What's going on? Didn't Marty say he'd given up on building those high-end condos?"

I slapped the paper on the table. "Of *course*, he told Luke that. He fooled all of us with that passionate speech about developing a bed and breakfast. Marty wanted Luke to relax and think he'd given up on buying the farm so he could swoop in."

She shuffled through more papers in the file. "This is almost worse."

She handed me a copy of a letter written by Ray to Marty: *Let Old Man Sinclair think you're going to make a big offer. Keep stringing him along. Once the farm goes into foreclosure, you'll get the property for pennies on the dollar. That's what your hundred thousand gets you!*

Lily grabbed my arm. "I'll make a copy of both papers for you to take to Luke. He has to get right on this and pay those taxes today." She checked the time on her phone. "The town office close at four thirty, so he only has an hour.

"What if he doesn't have the money?" I asked. "Would Luke be able to come up with a hundred thousand on such short notice?"

Lily was thinking fast and talking faster. "I'll loan it to him. Don't forget that Ray transferred a hundred thousand dollars into an account for me. I doubt he ever dreamed I'd use it to foil one of his schemes. Isn't it funny how karma can come back in unexpected ways?"

I folded the papers Lily shoved in my hand. "You should come with me."

Lily pushed me toward the door. "No. I'll keep

looking through these folders and meet you at the town office in a half hour. You need to come back with Luke or his dad. Hurry up, Dani."

The excitement-charged conversation must have filtered into Pip's nap because she was awake and out of the chair without my nudging her, eagerly waiting at the door, ready to help in any way possible.

As I hurried to the MG, I shot off a short text to Rose to let her know what was up. Next, a text to Luke that I was on my way to the farm with important information. Neither of them responded, which was irritating, but I didn't have the luxury of worrying.

Pip seemed to know something was different. I loved how she had tuned into my energy so quickly. Without hesitation, she jumped into the MG and took up her post, tapping her front paws on the dashboard in a kind of Morse code that I translated to mean time's a'wastin', Dani.

I guess the good traffic cops of Misty Harbor were on their donut breaks as I put the pedal to the metal and broke some speed barriers on my way over to Blueberry Acres, or I never would have made it in time.

CHAPTER TWENTY

Rose's Cadillac, parked behind the Blueberry Acres delivery truck, caught me by surprise when I pulled into the parking lot at the farm. Was something else going on here to complicate the pending disaster?

With Pip glued to my side like a sticky note, we hurried to the door, which opened before my knuckles had a chance for a second knock.

"Dani? What are you doing here?" Rose asked, surprise etched on her face.

"I was about to ask you the same thing. Is Luke here?" I stood on my tippy toes trying to peer behind her. Pip scooted right in without waiting for an invitation.

Rose glanced behind her then whispered,

"There's been an accident. Luke's wife is in the hospital, and he flew back to California to be with her. On his way to the airport, he called and asked me to stay with Spencer. He's been sitting in his chair with his head back and refuses to talk. I've known him my whole life, Dani, and I've never seen him like this. I'm at my wits end trying to get that stubborn old man to tell me what's going on."

Luke's gone? I didn't have time to sort out the jumble of emotions colliding through me at the moment. My eye was on the clock, or my mind's eye was and getting a hundred thousand dollars to the town office before Luke and Spencer lost the farm.

"It's worse than you can imagine," I said, out of breath from racing up to the office from the parking lot. I glanced at the window, half expecting to see Spencer's face looking at us. He wasn't. "Lily and I discovered some papers locked in Ray's desk that could mean the end of Blueberry Acres. Can I come in or should we continue this conversation outside?"

Rose stepped out with me and pulled the door closed. "What did you find?"

I handed the papers to Rose, wondering why the secrecy. Why wouldn't she let me into Spencer's house? She scanned the papers quickly, grasping the urgency instantly.

"Ray set this up? It's bad enough that Spencer was planning to sell the farm behind Luke's back but this?" She smacked the papers against her hand. "That man doesn't deserve to own anything in this town."

"Ray's dead, Rose. He *doesn't* own anything anymore. Lily is in charge of everything now. I think she's going to do a great job, but we don't have time for that discussion. If we show these papers to Spencer, they speak for themselves. Don't you think he'll understand that Ray and Marty planned to wait for him to lose the farm, leaving him with nothing? We have to get him to the town hall before they close."

I reached for the door, but Rose gripped my arm stopping me dead in my tracks.

"He'll understand … but he doesn't have this kind of money to clear up the bill on such short notice. This must be what has him in a deep depression. He couldn't bear to tell Luke what was happening because *he* doesn't have the money either."

I understood now. Rose was running interference for Spencer. But she was wasting time. "Lily has money," I said, trying to restrain myself from screaming my frustration. "Ray transferred it to her account, and she'll front it for Luke. Oh, Rose, Ray was up to his eyeballs in shady schemes, but this is the most urgent one to fix. Can you convince Spencer to come with us?"

Understanding brightened Rose's face. She grabbed my hand. "Come on. Together we'll get him there even if we have to tie him up and carry him."

I loved Rose's no-nonsense, quick-thinking solutions to difficult problems. They might not always be pretty, but nine times out of ten, her sharp thinking got the job done.

I followed her through the front hallway toward Spencer's comfortable sitting room with views that overlooked his blueberry fields. Memories of spending time here with Luke flooded my senses, but I shoved them away for now.

Spencer, eyes closed, and with Pip in his lap, sat in an overstuffed chair. "I've made a bloody mess of everything, Pip. At least Luke isn't here to witness what's going to happen today. Maybe he'll just stay in California. He'll probably never want to talk to me again."

Rose shook him out of his stupor. "Spencer! Get up and get your shoes on."

I knew he couldn't refuse that steely tone in her voice. I never could when I was younger and had to get moving so I wouldn't be late for school.

"Dani's here to take you to the town offices." Rose pulled him out of his chair before he had time to voice an argument. "She has a solution to your problem, and we don't have a minute to spare."

Poor Spencer. If Rose had knocked him over the head, I don't think he would have looked any more surprised. "But—"

"There's no time for *but's*, Spencer. Trust me, you don't want me to get any more upset with you than I already am. Why the heck didn't you come to your oldest friend and tell me what was going on?"

Spencer blinked several times. I looked away, not wanting him to know I saw the tears filling his eyes. "I can't pay the bill, Rose. It's hopeless."

Rose stopped, put her hands on her hips, and frowned at Spencer like a mother staring at a naughty child. She placed both of her hands on either side of his face and forced him to look at her. "Hopeless doesn't exist in my vocabulary. You should never give up without a fight. Now, I'm not going to tell you again—let's get a move on."

When we got to the front door, Spencer slid his feet into some old moccasins. Rose opened the door and, with her hand resting on his back, kept him moving.

"Get in my Cadillac. I know you love riding in the MG, but Pip has the passenger seat. We'll follow Dani and I'll explain everything."

"Rose." Spencer stopped next to the Cadillac. "You've been giving me orders for the last five minutes. When did you get so *bossy*?"

I laughed out loud, earning a glare from my grandmother.

"We've known each other for how long? Close to seventy years? I've *always* been bossy." She pulled the door open. "Now get in before your dawdling loses you this farm that's been in your family for generations."

I looked at Spencer, worried that he'd refuse to get in Rose's car.

He winked at me.

I grinned. "You can come with me if you'd rather. I'm sure Pip wouldn't mind sitting on your lap."

"Thanks, Dani. I'd better not. Who knows what

torture Rose would have in store if I don't follow her orders?" He saluted and settled onto the front seat of the Cadillac.

Rose slammed the door. As she walked around the back of her car, she paused next to me. "Thanks for figuring this out, Dani. Spencer's picking on me again, so I know he'll be fine." She shook her head. "That old obstinate farmer thinks it's a sin to ask for help. Now, get going before we run out of time. I'll follow you."

It was far too easy to zip along in Rose's spiffy MG, and before I realized it, a siren pierced through my thoughts and blue lights flashed in my rearview mirror.

I smacked my hands on the steering wheel, upset with my lack of vigilance, but looking for a scapegoat. "Why didn't you tell me to slow down, Pip?" Okay, that wasn't fair to blame her for my problem. As far as I could tell though, she didn't care because she looked at me and wagged her tail.

"License and registration, please."

Pip jumped on my lap and snapped at Detective Crenshaw's hand. I pulled her away from the open window before teeth met flesh, and I had a much bigger problem on my hands. "Sorry about that," I mumbled as I searched the glove compartment for Rose's registration.

Rose tooted as she drove past at, what I assumed, was exactly thirty-five miles an hour. She always drove the speed limit.

Spencer waved.

"I'm in a hurry, AJ." I handed him the registration.

"No kidding. Your license, too, Dani."

After I managed to push Pip onto the passenger seat, I dumped my bag on the floor and fished out my license. "Here you go." I smiled hoping it might put him in a more agreeable mood.

It didn't seem to have any affect. He just walked back to his car mumbling into his radio.

"Come on. Come on." My fingers drummed on the steering wheel, and I checked the rearview mirror every two seconds to see if AJ was done with whatever it was he was doing with my information. Checking to see if I was an escaped convict probably.

Finally, I heard his door open and the crunch of gravel as he returned to my window. "I'm giving you a warning, Dani. Slow down on these roads. I don't want to find you wrapped around a boulder."

"Thank you." I tried to sound contrite. "Oh, I have something important to tell you."

He waited.

"Lily and I overheard Rhonda say she was the one who trashed my apartment."

"Who was she talking to?"

"Frank Wilde." I couldn't see AJ's expression behind his sunglasses, but his eyebrows moved, and his forehead wrinkled

"Did she say why?"

"She thought Lily might have hidden some of Ray's contracts there. Lily and I were standing outside the office when she was talking to Frank about all this. Then, after she left, Lily discovered a locked drawer in Ray's desk with some interesting papers. Ray had advised Marty Fontaine to hold off on buying Blueberry Acres and just let it go into foreclosure so he could get it cheap." I refilled my lungs with a big intake of oxygen before I blurted out the rest of my information. "That's why I was in such a hurry. We, Rose and I, were taking Spencer to the town offices so he can pay his back taxes before it goes into foreclosure."

AJ stared at me as if his brain was trying to process everything I'd just told him.

"Can I go now?"

He smacked the top of the MG. "You're something else, Dani. I'll escort you."

I wasn't quite sure what he meant by "something else," but I wasn't going to argue about a police escort. It was the only way I'd make it in time.

CHAPTER TWENTY-ONE

The big rear end of Rose's Cadillac stuck into the street, forcing other cars in the parking lot of Misty Harbor's town offices to swerve around it. I hoped AJ didn't give her a ticket.

Thinking my luck had run out when I didn't see any parking spot, a car pulled out onto Main Street, leaving a space just big enough for the MG. I zipped into it and said, "Come on, Pip," not sure if dogs were allowed in the town offices.

"Mind your manners, keep a low profile, and maybe, just maybe, I'll be able to sneak you in. This is an emergency."

When I entered the building, I heard angry voices coming from the tax collector's office. "For a check of this size, it has to be certified, Mrs. Lemay. I can't take your word for it that the funds are available."

"Call the bank," I said as I entered the room. "For crying out loud, Martha, you've known Lily since she was a baby and you've known Spencer since you two went to kindergarten together. Since when does the town of Misty Harbor refuse to take a hundred grand from one of the town's business-women to save a farm that everyone loves?"

Martha's tight, grey curls did not budge when she looked up with a grim line across her mouth. "We have rules to follow, Ms. Mackenzie, as I've already explained to these people." She crossed her arms and glared at me to defy her.

Spencer leaned on Martha's desk. "Dani's right," he said in a soothing voice. "Do you want it on your conscience when my blueberry bushes are yanked out? Bulldozed under and replaced with fancy condos bringing in hordes of people who don't really care about Misty Harbor? Is that what you want, Martha? Because, if you do, I'll walk out of here and start packing my bags."

Silence settled in every nook and cranny of the old office as I held my breath. Everyone else in the busy department must have been doing the same thing, because you could have heard a pin drop. Or a ripe blueberry.

Martha's lip quivered and the floor creaked when she shuffled back a step. She dropped her arms; her shoulders sagged. "No, Spencer, I don't want that. But I don't want to lose my job."

"You won't. Lily's money is as good as gold. This check won't bounce." He held it out to Martha.

She looked doubtful and checked over her shoulder as though some tax collector was ready to pounce on her. Then she gave the imaginary supervisor a defiant smirk and said, "Okay then."

She took the check from Spencer and stamped the overdue tax bill as paid in full. "I didn't know about the condos. That would ruin our little town."

Rose, Lily, and I waited until we walked out of the office to hug and high five each other. Spencer stayed behind to chat a little longer with Martha.

"Did you get a ticket?" Rose asked me. "I guess I'll have to take those keys away from you for your own darn good. And, to think I was planning to give you that car." She shook her head.

"Really? Pip loves the MG. How about you give

it to her, and I'll just be, you know, her personal driver? Have you seen how she puts her front paws on the dash, so she doesn't miss a thing?"

Rose chuckled, and I knew she'd only been giving me a hard time. I pumped my fist. "Did you hear that, Pipster? We saved Blueberry Acres *and* we got us a sleek set of wheels."

"Misty Harbor is in trouble now." I spun around to see AJ laughing at me. "You managed to save Blueberry Acres?"

"Lily did." I couldn't take the credit and made sure AJ understood this was all Lily's doing. I smiled at her. "It's kind of ironic that Ray's parting gift to you undermined one of his last schemes."

"Well congratulations, Lily," AJ said. "Now, how about you two come to my office with those papers you told me about. I want to take a look at what you found. Dani rattled off that information so fast I couldn't keep it all straight."

"I'll wait for Spencer," Rose said to me. "You and Lily go with AJ, and I'll have dinner ready when you get done."

"You might want to move your car, Rose," AJ said. "Just this once, I'll pretend I didn't see that you're parked illegally."

As much as I wanted to head back to Ray's office and go through more of his papers, I couldn't say no to AJ's request. It wasn't really the kind of question that left any room for a no answer. I jumped into Lily's car so we could talk on the way to the police station.

Pip seemed to love all this running around lifestyle I'd dragged her into. At least, she didn't complain, so I took that as a positive. "Did you find anything else, Lil?"

"Nothing as earth shattering as the papers about the farm and the funeral home, but I've barely scratched the surface of everything in Ray's office. It's locked up nice and tight now, so no one else can snoop around."

"Good thinking."

"How does AJ know we found some papers?" she asked as she headed for the police station.

"When he pulled me over for speeding . . ."

"Wait, speeding?"

"Keep your eyes on the road," I said, "I'll explain later. For now, it all spilled out in my explanation on why I was in such a hurry to get into town. He ended up giving me an escort once he heard about the foreclosure problem. I guess now he wants to see everything with his own eyes and not take my word that I wasn't trying to pull some-thing over on him."

"Makes sense. Did you tell him about Rhonda trashing your apartment?"

"Uh-huh."

Lily turned into the police station parking lot, pulling into a space next to a black BMW.

I gave it a squint. "I've seen that car before. It almost ran me off the road this morning." It took me a minute to replay the moment. "Ava was driving. I wonder what she's doing here."

Lily reached behind her seat for her bag. "Maybe she's turning herself in as Ray's killer."

I scoffed and came up with a more likely scenario. "Maybe that whole story she told us about buying all that stuff at Creative Designs was just that, a story. It would be easy enough to check if she has receipts." I opened my door. "Ready, Pip?"

"It cracks me up how you talk to that dog like she's a person, Dani. Do you ever expect her to answer you?"

I looked at Lily over the hood of her car. "She answers me all the time—a tail wag means she agrees with me, a lick on my chin means I'm right, and a woof means—"

"Shut the door and let's get this over with?" Lily said with an eye roll.

"I haven't figured that one out yet. But, seriously, Lil, I think she does understand me when I'm talking to her. She's smart and a fierce little bundle of Ms. Cool."

"I suppose she's coming in with us?"

Pip looked at Lily and wagged her tail. "See? She's telling you that there's no way she's missing any of this action."

Lily pushed her lower lip into a pretend pout. "I've been displaced by a white, ten-pound-terrier with brown ears, brown circles around her eyes, and a big attitude." Lily pretended to be annoyed but I knew she loved Pip, too. Just not as much as I did.

Ava walked out of the station and wobbled down the steps to the sidewalk. Her four-inch-heels looked deadly enough to kill someone—herself most likely when she twisted her ankle, fell, and broke her neck. If she managed to stay vertical for long enough, I might be nice to her.

"What's up, Ava?" Her startled reaction broke her concentration and almost made her lose her balance.

"Oh, it's *you* two."

I took that as a compliment.

"You're like a bad nightmare that keeps popping up when I least expect it. And, I don't even have Marty here for support. He was all like, 'I have some important stuff do in New York, but you can't come.' And then, that rude detective called me in to explain why Marty left." She threw her arms up in the air. "Apparently, he thinks that *I'm* supposed to keep my eyes on Marty every minute. I don't think so, is what I told him. I have my yoga, my spa, my hair appointment, and my nails to take care of. Marty had his own stuff to do."

She stopped in front of us but was careful to leave enough space so Pip couldn't reach her. I thought her rant was over. I tried to wrap my head around what it really meant that Marty left town because in my opinion, it didn't bode well for him.

"You know what the worst part is?" she continued.

"You broke a nail?" I couldn't resist.

Before she realized it was a gotcha, Ava held both hands up and checked. "No," she snarled, snapping her hands back down, "I didn't. The worst part is, that detective told me not to leave. What am I supposed to do in this backwards town?"

"Well . . ." I paused to be sure she was paying attention. "Sometimes, we like to count the wet rocks on the beach during low tide or another fun thing is to sit very quietly until a seagull poops on our head." Somehow, I'd managed to get that out with a straight face.

Lily sucked both lips in between her teeth, but I still heard a snort. Pip's little tail wagged so fast her whole butt joined the party.

Ava stared at me for so long I had to wonder if maybe I did have seagull poop on my head. "That's disgusting," she said, then wobbled to her car and yanked the door open.

"Really, Dani? Was that necessary?" Lily gave me a side eye.

"What? I can't have a little fun with out-of-towners? She has no trouble insulting us." I elbowed Lily. "Besides, you're laughing. You thought it was funny."

We walked into the station, letting out random giggles at Ava's expense to help ease the tension swirling around from the day's events. Pip wiggled until I put her down, and she sniffed around the police station while we waited for AJ. The only one who seemed to mind Pip's wandering was Trouble, the police station's one-eyed tabby cat. He'd moved in about a year earlier taking over the job as official meet and greeter. Apparently, Trouble preferred the two-legged variety of visitors.

When Pip put her front feet out and her rear end up in her play bow position, Trouble hissed and swatted. Pip seemed to think was a new activity. When it escalated into a game of chase, Trouble ended up at the top of the file cabinets, tail switching, hair on end, and growling.

By the time AJ found us, I had Pip securely tucked under my arm again, both of us looking cute and innocent. The detective looked at Trouble and then at Pip before he directed his question to me. "What was that awful yowl I heard a minute ago?"

I shrugged. "Trouble was saying hello." From the look AJ gave me, I suspected he knew there was more to the story, but he left it at that.

"Come on back to my office," he said, leading the way past interrogation rooms and a heavy metal door that gave me the chills as I imagined the cells with bars behind it. AJ extended his hand for us to enter first and closed the door when we were inside. Every surface was piled with files and papers that AJ managed to shuffle around until he had uncovered two metal folding chairs for us.

I held Pip in my lap, but she had other ideas, and jumped down to go exploring.

"So," AJ said, stepping over a stack of files and collapsing into his swivel desk chair, "did you bring the papers you told me about?"

Lily opened her bag, took out a folder, and handed it to AJ. "I made copies so you can keep these. One is about Blueberry Acres and the other is a sale agreement to sell the funeral home building."

While AJ took his time studying the documents, I took note of his office décor, the out-of-date calendar on the wall next to a framed photo of AJ fishing with Ray. A happier time between those two I imagined. I gave him my attention when he said, "This is interesting. Marty Fontaine paid Ray a hundred thousand dollars." He looked at Lily. "Did you know about any of this?"

Lily shook her head. "None of it, AJ. From what I discovered while searching Ray's office today, Ray didn't play by the rules and that document you're looking at now about selling the funeral home building has my signature on it. But I didn't sign it. It's a forgery."

"Are you positive?"

Lily's eyes blazed when she insisted, "I did *not* sign that document. The way I see it, Ray planned to sell the property and whisk me away on the trip he promised, and I would never have known the difference."

AJ pursed his lips, considering his next question. "Has Frank mentioned this sale to you?"

"Yes. He and Rhonda were in Ray's office before Dani and I arrived. I think they were looking for the contract."

"That's right," I said. "That's when we heard Rhonda tell Frank that she searched my apartment for it. What are you going to do, AJ?"

He sat back before answering. "Make a visit to the Wilde brothers to find out what's going on with this contract and have a little chat with Rhonda, too."

I cautioned AJ. "There's some kind of romance going on between Frank and Rhonda. We caught them all smoochy and huggy but they tried to pull apart real fast when they realized we were watching," I said. "Did you identify either of those earrings yet? I wonder if Frank and Rhonda decided to wear matching diamond stars."

AJ looked thoughtful and shook his head. "Not yet. I'm hoping that whoever lost either earring might come to the police station asking about it."

"And if no one comes asking about a diamond

earring…maybe, that's just as incriminating, don't you think?" If *I'd* lost it at the scene of a murder, I'd stay as far away as possible from asking about it and connecting myself to a clue.

A smile was AJ's answer.

CHAPTER TWENTY-TWO

L ily drove me back to the MG and followed me to Sea Breeze for a well-earned meal, wine, and girl talk since she was spending the night.

Pip must have been tired because she curled up on the front seat instead of keeping watch through the windshield. I found the sensitive spot under her ear and gave it a few scratches. "You're great company, Pipster. Thanks for sticking with me."

Her little tail slapped on the seat telling me she agreed. Or, at least, she liked the sound of my voice.

The mouthwatering aromas when I stepped through the front door of Sea Breeze filled my senses with a mixture of fresh bread, roasted vegetables, and a hint of something sweet. I let my nose lead the way while my stomach growled with anticipation.

Pip, refreshed from her nap, dashed through the house and beat both Lily and me to the coziest room in the house. Rose must have anticipated our needs since she had wine glasses set out and a plate with crackers and cheese ready.

"You're the best, Rose." I leaned close and brushed my lips against her soft cheek. "I could get used to this, you know."

Rose waved her spatula in my direction. "You don't have to live in that apartment. Move in with me whenever you want. I like the company. Pip will be happier here I'm sure, and I won't charge you any rent."

I stared out the window at the darkening shadows on the bay, deciding I had the best life this side of heaven. At least when I visited Rose. "You don't charge me rent now, and I only have to roll out of bed and walk down the stairs to get to the diner."

Rose turned back to her stove and finished turning her pan of sausage and vegetables. "You have a reliable car now so you could stay here."

It was a tempting offer. "I'll think about it. With my apartment off limits, this can be the practice run to see if we get sick of each other." I sliced a couple of pieces of cheddar cheese, layered them on crackers, and offered one to Lily.

The front door opened. "Hello?"

"In the kitchen, Spencer." Rose lowered her voice. "I told him to join us for dinner. He's relieved about the farm, but worried about what Luke is going through with Jennifer in intensive care. It doesn't look good for her."

Spencer walked in, handing a bottle of red wine to Rose. His face, drawn with what I could only assume was worry, made him look older than his mid-seventies age.

"How is Luke doing?" I asked, not sure if he'd want to talk or not but giving him the opportunity to do either.

"Thanks for asking, Dani. To be honest, I don't know. I don't think he's gotten past the shock and the trip and the exhaustion yet. All we can do is hope for the best and wait."

Rose had the wine opened, poured, and handed filled glasses to each of us. She tipped her glass toward Spencer. "I'm glad you've joined us. It's better to have company than be alone at a time like this."

He nodded and sat at Rose's kitchen nook,

staring out the window—with us in body but his thoughts had to be three thousand miles away.

"Did you learn anything from AJ?" Rose asked.

I got silverware out and set the table in the dining room while Rose portioned the food onto plates. "We showed him the papers Lily found in Ray's office. He was especially interested in the agreement to sell the funeral home property with Lily's forged signature.

"Are you going to sell, Lily?" Rose carried two plates to the table and returned for the other two.

"Both Frank and Nick have already tried to talk about a sale. I probably will sell, but I'm not going to make any big decisions this soon. First, I have to understand what I actually own."

Rose tapped Spencer on his shoulder. "Are you going to sit with us?"

"If you don't mind, I'm not very hungry. I'll sit here and keep Pip company." Spencer's hand rested on the terrier, who seemed to be quite happy with the arrangement.

I sipped my wine, forcing myself to make it last. "We bumped into Ava, too, and she told us that Marty has skipped town."

"Really?"

"Yeah and she's not too happy that AJ told her she had to stay here."

"I don't think Marty killed Ray," Lily said. "He was on track to get Blueberry Acres for a song. What would he gain from killing Ray?"

"That's a good point. He already gave Ray a hundred grand and he had all sorts of grandiose plans. Why kill the one person who seemed to be on his side?" I asked.

Rose nodded agreement. "And Ava has an alibi."

I lowered my voice so Spencer wouldn't hear my next comment. "What if Luke found out what Ray and Marty were up to with Blueberry Acres? He had the perfect opportunity to kill Ray and, to be honest, I couldn't blame him if he did. And now he's gone."

"He's been cleared." Spencer's voice surprised me. "The owner of a stop he made in Glendale came forward and said he saw Luke's delivery truck around eleven. So, he couldn't have been in Misty Harbor when Ray was murdered. It's a good thing I didn't know what was going on or I would have taken care of Ray myself. Sorry, Lily, but your husband was no good, only out for himself, and you're better off without someone like that."

"That's great news, Spencer." I was glad to know that Luke's name was cleared.

Rose patted the chair next to her. "Sit down, Spencer. I'll reheat your food."

We all urged him to join us and he finally relented and took a place at the table. His appetite seemed to have miraculously returned when Rose set his plate in front of him, judging from the way he dug into the sausages. When he caught a breath, he said, "Luke told me what that guy Marty said about turning the farmhouse into a bed and break-fast or an Inn, can't remember which it was." He took a swig of his wine and added, "But I kind of like the idea. When Luke gets back, I want to have a serious talk with him about some changes at the farm before we run into another cash flow problem."

Then he tucked into his meal again to catch up with the rest of us.

"You know, Spencer—" Lily started.

He stopped her with the wine glass in his hand. "Before you say anything else, Lily. I will pay you back. I don't take handouts."

She grinned and nodded her head. "Fair enough. But what I was going to say is that maybe we can work out some kind of deal. I like the idea of running an inn. When you're ready to talk seriously, would you give me the first option to make an offer?"

Spencer put his fork down. His nostrils flared in that way they do when you're trying to hold your emotions back. "It's a deal, Lily. I can't think of anyone I'd rather work with."

I glanced at Rose and saw the teary glaze over her eyes, too. It always stuns me when something good comes from something bad. Everything might just work out for Blueberry Acres after all. "Is there any dessert?" I asked to keep the party from getting to soppy.

Rose gave me one of her long-suffering chuckles. "You and your sweet tooth, Dani. How about you help me get it."

I followed her into the kitchen with a stack of dirty dishes I gathered on my way around the table. "I'm not sure we can pop open the champagne yet," I said, unloading them into the sink, "but I'm excited that Lily and Spencer seem to be working toward a common goal."

Rose had stacked dessert plates and bustled around the kitchen while I shared my concerns. "I never imagined her running an inn, but you know, she'd be darn good at it. She's organized, a hard worker, and loves interacting with people. You know I hate to complain, but I don't know how I'll manage at the diner without her."

I guess Rose didn't take my worries seriously at the moment. She had more of a let's-wait-and-see-what-happens attitude. She busied herself removing the cover from a big pan of blueberry crisp.

"You brought blueberries and I had to do *something* with them," she explained as if serving blueberry crisp was a problem. "There's ice cream in the freezer, too. We might as well go all out and have the works."

I didn't object.

When I returned to the dining room with dessert plates and the ice cream, I heard Spencer say, "Luke wants to move back to Misty Harbor but Jennifer won't leave California. When he came back, I think it was kind of a trial separation but now…"

He left the rest unsaid because we all knew that Luke would never leave Jennifer now while she was injured and needed him most. I admired his loyalty but seeing him again made this latest separation even more painful.

As we were passing the dessert, Spencer's phone interrupted our conversation.

One look at his face though, and a sense of dread came over us.

He answered in monosyllables that didn't give us much of a clue before he hung up.

He sat staring at his phone for a moment, the color draining from his face. Then he looked up at the ceiling, searching for words or trying to find his voice. I'm not sure what was going through his mind, I could only imagine. He said simply, "Jennifer died. Luke will call again in the morning." What else was there to say when your loved one's world is suddenly torn apart?

We ate dessert with the clink of forks on our plates the only sound as shock enveloped us all.

Pip must have sensed our sadness. She jumped on Spencer's lap with an understanding that he needed her attention the most.

Pip—the perfect companion.

CHAPTER TWENTY-THREE

Rain pinging on the window woke me Wednesday morning. The soothing pitter-patter almost lulled me back to sleep, but Pip saw me stretch and yawn, and with a lick of my cheek, she let me know it was time to get up.

"Pip," I groaned, "go away," and rolled over on my side, but that only encouraged her. She dug under the blankets and nudged me with her nose until I whined, "Okay. Okay. Did Rose send you up here to drag me out of bed?"

Pip jumped on top of me and chased her stubby tail up and down the length of me until she had me crying with laughter. "Now you've added a morning giggle to your bag of tricks, Pippy?"

I couldn't put it off any longer, so I slid out from

under the soft sheets and pulled a flannel shirt on to ward off the moist, chilly morning air and followed Pip downstairs.

Rose was in her usual spot on the couch, but instead of enjoying a view of Blueberry Bay, her window was blocked by a thick soup of fog.

"I've been thinking," Rose said as she sipped her coffee. "I'm wondering if Rhonda thought she had the most to gain with her brother out of the way."

I glanced her way. "Good morning to you, Rose. Love waking up to talk of murder before I've had my coffee."

"Oh, sorry, dear. Good morning, but you know, it was a big gamble on Rhonda's part if she did kill him, but maybe she thought as the remaining sibling she could bully Lily into turning the business over to her. Or at least, take control and slip right into Ray's shoes."

I shook my head. That's Rose, a dog with a bone when she's getting her head around something I thought as I padded past her toward the kitchen. "I need a few more minutes for my brain to wake up before I settle down for this conversation. How about I refill your coffee while I get my own mug."

Rose held her mug out. "Don't forget to give Pip her breakfast while you're in the kitchen. She's been eyeing me for the last hour. That's why I sent her upstairs to get you."

"And I thought it was because you were lonely and couldn't wait for my companionship," I teased.

Rose did a sitting yoga stretch – I know because I heard her joints crack – and called after me, "I do enjoy having you here, Dani. I hope you're serious about considering my offer to move in. It would be good for all three of us. Right, Pip?"

Of course, the little traitor that she was, wagged her tail as she raced around my feet. "Not fair, you two are ganging up against me." I had to admit that I liked the idea more and more. But I wanted to be one hundred percent sure that Rose wouldn't resent losing her privacy. "Come on Pip. Or, do I have to serve your breakfast in a little silver dish?"

Pip followed me to her bowl where I poured in her kibble. "Good, you aren't too fashionable to eat like a normal dog."

There was just enough coffee left for two servings. I returned to Rose with the mugs, leaving Pip to finish her breakfast.

I plopped down in a comfy chair opposite Rose and pondered her theory while I let caffeine work its wonders on my still sleepy brain. "Okay," I said after my mug was half gone, "Rhonda. That's an interesting theory and if the earring found in the diner turns out to be hers, I would say it looks bad. But kill her own brother?"

Rose cocked an eyebrow at me. "The Lemay's are *not* a close family. They've always been highly competitive and cutthroat while they clawed their way to the top of the heap. It's not a stretch to imagine Rhonda becoming so obsessed, so greedy, that she'd stop at nothing."

I considered that scenario as I swirled the last of my coffee. "She may have been biding her time for Ray and Lily to finalize the divorce, which was pushed aside with talk of reconciliation. I'm sure she wasn't happy about that. But what about Frank?"

"Frank?" she said as though she'd never heard the name before.

"Yeah," I explained. "Doesn't it seem more likely that Rhonda would talk *him* into committing the crime, so her hands stayed clean?"

I could see the wheels turning in Rose's head, so I pressed on. "You know, something like: if you love me, you'll kill my brother for me to prove it." I was being sarcastic but who knew what went on in the name of love? "Another thing, we don't know who signed Lily's name on that sales agreement."

"Do you think Rhonda forged the signature?"

I shrugged. "I don't know. What I do know is that Rhonda and Frank are involved with each other romantically and the way they were searching Ray's office, I have to assume that they were in on some mischief together."

I could see I had Rose's agreement on that.

"Frank and Nick didn't want to keep renting from Ray. And, those two earrings have to be key to solving the crime."

As we sat and talked, the thinning fog began to create ghostlike silhouettes over the bay. I loved how the view could transform from a dreamy quality that blurred reality and in another hour or so, a vivid scene emerged of boats, birds, and a brilliant blue sky.

"What about Nick?" Rose asked.

"What *about* him?"

"Was he involved in the phony real estate contract with Ray? Would he benefit from Ray's death?"

I thought about that angle. "Well, of course he'd benefit as a partner in Two Wilde Funeral Home if the real estate transition went through. Now that you mention him, I don't remember seeing his name on that paper. I wonder why he was kept out of the loop?"

Rose snapped her finger in an, I've-got-it moment, and Pip came running out of the kitchen, I guess to see what she was missing. The gleam in Rose's eyes told me she was on to something.

"I think he's the one you and Lily should talk to. Show him that contract and see how he reacts, but don't let Frank know what you're doing. Don't let them coordinate their story."

I finished my coffee and stretched. "Shouldn't AJ be doing all this?"

"Good point and my guess is that he's also looking at every angle but not the way you and Lily would. Different eyes; different perspective. Lily can always say she needs to put the final touches on the funeral, so her visit looks innocent. Whereas if AJ barges in, those two brothers will be on the defensive, closing up tighter than a lobster claw clamping on its prey."

Rose took a deep breath and flexed her ankles, signaling me she was done with this detective work. "Go wake Lily," she said. "I don't know how anyone can sleep this late."

"*Scandalous*. It's seven o'clock already? The day's almost over."

Rose looked down her nose at me. "Don't get sassy, Dani."

And that was why I wasn't sure living with Rose would be a good decision. I loved hanging out with her, but she liked things *her* way on *her* schedule. I couldn't blame her. I was exactly the same way. Would we clash too much if I moved in? A big part of me would love to live at Sea Breeze and be out of town where my neighbors, and let's face it, in that small town everyone was my neighbor, had their nose in my business. Here, on the other hand, Rose could scrutinize every little thing I did. Which would be harder to deal with? That was my problem. I didn't know.

Pip leaped to the back of the couch, tearing me away from having to make this decision for now. Her tail wagged furiously, her nose twitched, and her ears pricked toward the doorway indicating that *something* was about to happen.

By the time my ears picked up the sounds of scuffing, Lily was dragging herself in from the bedroom. I turned my head and caught her stretching from side to side and over her head, releasing a ripple of cracks in what looked to be an attempt to loosen up her stiff muscles.

"Mornin' Rose, Dani. Any coffee left?" She

bent over and scratched behind Pip's ear as we greeted her.

"I'll make another pot," I said.

"Thanks, Dani." She fell into the nearest chair, clearly not rested, at least to my eyes, from her night's sleep."

"What's up, Lil? You look like you had a restless night."

She ran her hands over her face and even though dark circles outlined her eyes, nothing could take away her natural beauty. She let out a pitiful sigh and pleaded, "Will you come to the funeral home with me today, Dani?"

How could I say no? "Sure, but why?" She didn't know about the plan Rose and I cooked up.

"This funeral has me on edge. I want to discuss the refreshments with Frank and Nick for Sunday. It hit me that I need to offer something after Ray's funeral. Right?"

The stress of the last few days had etched itself in a shadow of sadness around her mouth. "Sure, I'll come with you. Let's all go in the kitchen for some breakfast and talk about your plans."

Rose got up to join us. "Yes, I think Ray would approve of you having a reception afterwards," she said. "We could make meat, veggie, and cheese platters, cookies, and a variety of salads and invite everyone who is interested, to come here afterwards. How does that sound?"

"I don't want to impose," Lily said somewhat hesitantly. "But it probably won't be too many people."

Rose put her arms around Lily in a gentle embrace. "Lily, you know I wouldn't offer if I didn't want to do this, so don't think for one minute that helping you is an imposition. But, just to be clear, I'm doing it for you, not Ray."

"All right, then." Lily tapped my arm. "Do you have enough of your blueberry cordial to make a sparkling punch?"

I didn't want to waste my cordial on Ray's relatives, but I couldn't say no to Lily. "It all depends. I don't know if my little stash made it through the destruction at the diner or whether AJ will even let me go in to get any survivors."

Lily pulled the refrigerator door open and scoffed at my concern. "He already let you in once so I'm sure he'll agree to this. Ray was his best friend even if he told me they weren't really close lately." Then she bent over to check the contents before lifting her head over the door. "Can I help myself to whatever is in here, Rose?"

"Of course, and fix something for us too, while you're at it. I don't want your short-order cooking skills to get rusty while the diner is closed." Rose sat in the kitchen nook, kitty-corner to the seat Pip adopted as hers—the prime spot in front of the window.

With the fog lifting, Blueberry Bay's early visitors came into view. A few lobster boats cut through the water checking their traps. Small boats moored at their buoys bobbed in a gentle rhythm with the wave action and above it all, the seagulls soared parallel to the beach. I'd be crazy to say no to this view every morning I told myself.

Lily snapped her fingers in my face. "Earth to Dani, scrambled or fried?"

"Scrambled. I'll be on toast duty."

As soon as the coffee pot had finished dripping, a loud bang on the front door got Pip yipping and charging toward the intruder.

"Isn't it too early for a visitor?" I moaned. I liked our little group of three, or four, not meaning to forget to count Pip.

"Add more eggs to the pan, Lily," Rose said, as she left the kitchen, following Pip to the door.

I resented this intrusion but, of course, Lily cracked more eggs.

CHAPTER TWENTY-FOUR

AJ twisted his hat in his hands, an apologetic expression on his face as he gave his report.

"Sorry to intrude so early but I wanted to let you know that we're done in the Little Dog Diner and you're free to go back and start cleaning up."

"Well come on into the kitchen," I said. He seemed afraid to step over the threshold as if maybe the floors had just been mopped.

"Like I told Dani already," he said, moving up to the island, "I can probably round up some help with cleanup. We took lots of photos, but if you see anything unusual or find anything missing, let me know. Of course, I had to take the rolling pin as evidence."

I handed AJ a mug of coffee, thinking it might

help him relax a little or it might do the opposite and kick his nerves into high gear.

Hmm, but what about *my* nerves. "That should be good news," I said, "but I've got mixed feelings about going back inside." Just thinking about the scene inside the diner brought back the memory of seeing Ray's dead body on the floor. Somehow, I'd have to figure out how to erase that image.

AJ looked from Lily to me and said, "That's why I think you should have someone else do the cleanup. Once the diner looks like new again, it will be easier to move forward."

"Well, it didn't exactly look new even on the best of days," I countered, "but I get your meaning." However, I still wasn't convinced.

Rose took her seat at the window nook and, as usual, brought a rational note to the conversation. "AJ is right, Dani. Just check if any of your blueberry cordial survived and forget about everything else. I'll hire a crew to take care of the cleanup. Besides, I've made up my mind to gut the place and do a complete remodel. This is as good an excuse as I'll ever have and it's probably long overdue anyway. The insurance settlement will help to cover some of the renovation expenses."

AJ leaned against the counter and sipped his coffee. "What's the blueberry cordial for?"

"A reception after Ray's funeral," I said. "Here at Sea Breeze. Lily wants to have a touch of local flavor."

Mention of the funeral made me wonder how Luke was coping with the loss of his wife. "Did you hear the news about Luke's wife?"

AJ's hand stopped midway toward his lips.

"She died last night."

He let out a deep sigh. "I'm really sorry to hear that. Luke has had a lot fall in his lap lately. I'm glad his alibi checked out so at least he doesn't have to rush back here as a murder suspect."

A pall fell over the kitchen, and though the loss of Luke's wife was a tragedy, we had to move on for the moment. I knew we would all be there for him when he returned to Misty Harbor.

"Speaking of suspects," I said to deftly change the subject, "what about that Marty Fontaine guy leaving town? I bumped into his wife yesterday." A chuckle bubbled out. "You managed to ruin *her* plans. The way she explained it, you might have ruined her whole life when you told her she had to stay in Misty Harbor."

AJ scowled. "To be honest? I'll be glad when they both leave town, and I never have to lay eyes on them again. People like the Fontaines don't fit in our town with their uppity attitudes and big ideas to develop every square inch of land."

"Oh?" I said, surprised. "Are they cleared as suspects?" If that were true, the suspect list was shrinking quickly. I popped four pieces of bread into the toaster and pushed the lever down.

"Ava spent a couple of hours shopping when Creative Designs opened, asking questions and buying all sorts of items. Her alibi checks out. Marty didn't stay with her but at this point there isn't a strong motive for him to have killed Ray. Since Ray was working with him to steal Blueberry Acres from Spencer, why would he want Ray dead? Did I miss something else with him?" AJ asked.

"Only that Ava told me Ray sold Marty a worthless piece of land. Did you find anymore paperwork involving those two, Lil?" I buttered the toast and checked to see if the eggs were ready.

"Not yet." Lily turned the burner off and moved the pan of eggs off the heat. "There's plenty of scrambled eggs if you want a quick bite, AJ."

He held up his hand. "Thanks, but I'm good.

Keep looking through those papers, okay? I plan to question Marty some more when he returns. His wife promised it would be later today, and I hope she's right. It feels like I'm heading into a bunch of dead ends. I had high hopes that the rolling pin and that earring would connect *someone* to the murder but so far, no one has asked about a missing diamond earring and the lab results …" he made a circle with his thumb and forefinger, "less than helpful. Is there any chance the earring was in the diner the day *before* the murder? Maybe someone bought it at Creative Designs then went to eat at the diner and dropped it, but it wasn't discovered until *after* Ray was killed?"

"Unlikely," Rose said and shook her head for emphasis. "The diner gets a thorough cleaning every night—floors swept *and* washed. I don't think it would be possible for an earring, or anything else, to be on the floor and not get discovered by the end of the day."

"Okay, thanks, ladies." AJ put his mug in the sink and headed for the doorway. "You've given me some angles to think about. I have to head back to town; just wanted to let you know about the diner. I'll let myself out."

Lily divided the eggs onto three plates, and I

added the buttered toast before we joined Rose and Pip at the kitchen nook. "Do you think he came here to tell us about the diner or ask that question about whether the earring could have been on the floor before the murder?"

I took a bite of toast covered with eggs.

"Both," Rose said, "but I think the earring question was important. We all made the *assumption* that the earring belonged to the killer because we know the diner is thoroughly cleaned every night. The diner was closed the day of the murder so no was inside except Ray and the murderer. I'm not even counting you two when you got the blueberry cordial because, well, that's a no brainer since neither of you killed him. AJ has to rule out the possibility that someone *besides* the killer dropped the earring during the murder. It's very unlikely that it belongs to anyone but the killer. Right?"

I drummed my fingers on the table as I tried to work through various possibilities. "Luke and Ava have alibis. AJ doesn't think Marty has a strong motive so let's forget about him for now. That sparkly diamond earring didn't walk into the diner by itself, and Pip sure as heck didn't lose it. That leaves Rhonda or Frank, who both lost an earring.

One was lost at the funeral home and one in the diner. Are you with me?"

At the sound of her name, Pip lifted her head, but she didn't wag her tail or bark. I think she was waiting for me to reveal the murderer. I wished I could.

Rose and Lily each gave me a big head nod to indicate they were on the same page; so I continued.

"Don't you think it makes the most sense that Frank lost *his* earring while he was getting Ray all set in the casket for the fake funeral? So, whose earring was found at the murder scene at the Little Dog Diner?"

Rose suggested a new idea. "We've been so focused on the earring, what if the murderer *didn't* drop it?" she asked. "I told AJ I was sure the earring would have been swept up if it had been lost the day before the murder, but in reality, it's *possible* it was already there, just not likely. So, I think a new question is, if we forget about the earring for a minute, who else could have been in the diner with Ray? I think Marty did have a motive to kill Ray and what about Nick? If Frank is a suspect, his brother should be too, in my opinion."

I looked at Lily. "What do *you* think? You know the Wilde brothers better than we do."

She shrugged her shoulders with an *I-don't-know* gesture. "Nick's a quiet guy. He's always in the background with his head down working while Frank is more the face of the company. Maybe he's jealous? I've never seen them argue or fight, though." She scooted over to the counter and grabbed her purse, found a dollar and slapped it on the table. "I put my money on Rhonda. She was *always* jealous of Ray. Anyone care to make a bet on someone else? Frank, Marty, or Nick?"

I fished a dollar from my pocket and threw it on the table. "My money's on Frank because I think Rhonda would convince him to do her dirty work. What about you, Rose?"

"I don't bet, but I think you've both spun interesting scenarios. Since you're going to the funeral home to discuss more details for Ray's funeral, poke around with some questions about the earring and see what you can discover. I'll be at my office working on this article."

I wiped up the last of Lily's creamy, perfectly seasoned scrambled eggs with my toast and washed it all down with the rest of my coffee. "Well, that hit the spot. When do you want to leave, Lil?"

"How about a half hour? If we stop at the diner first to get the blueberry cordial, then go to the funeral home, we'll be there around nine. We should be able to find one or both of the brothers even though I didn't make an appointment." Lily grinned. "I like the idea of catching them off guard."

I stacked the breakfast dishes and carried them to the sink. "That works for me."

"Don't worry about the dishes," Rose said. "I'll put everything in the dishwasher then head to my office." She waved her hands and shooed both of us out of her way.

It didn't take long for Lily to meet me by the front door, showered, wet hair braided, and dressed in her black leggings and cream-colored rayon tunic.

I looked down at my hot pink capris and my Little Dog Diner t-shirt with a bowl of steamin' clam chowdah decorating the front. "Do I have to change? You look so ... ready for a business meeting or something."

Lily laughed. "You'll keep Frank and Nick off balance with your outfit, which is exactly what we want."

I slapped my leg. "Come on Pip. We're heading off on another adventure."

Pip pranced to the front door sporting a rainbow-colored bandana. Apparently, Rose had an endless supply to give Pip a splash of color and dash of flair to match her mood each day.

"Aren't we the trio?" I said as I opened the door.

CHAPTER TWENTY-FIVE

With Pip in her co-pilot spot, I was extra careful to stay under the speed limit as I drove into Misty Harbor. The next time I got pulled over, I doubted I'd get off with just a warning. I'd surely get a ticket thrown in my pitiful face.

The fog had lifted but clouds hung low in the sky, threatening a dreary day with the possibility of rain. I parked in front of the diner, which, at least from the outside, looked pretty normal. Thankfully, the police had pulled up all their yellow crime tape, but they had completely trampled our narrow strip of grass.

Lily and I took the shortest path to the cabinet with the blueberry cordial, the side door.

"Are you ready?" Lily asked me. "I don't have

much of a memory beyond Ray's body on the floor. I blacked out everything else and then took off. Do you want to stay out here? I don't mind going in by myself."

I sucked in a breath for bravery. "I can do it," I said. I felt Pip lean against my leg. She either sensed my anxieties or she had her own bad memories to deal with. I picked her up.

Lily opened the door and gasped.

"What?" My heart pounded.

"I can't believe this colossal mess. Rose made the right decision to gut the place and remodel. There isn't much worth salvaging." Lily turned in a circle. "Someone must have just pushed everything off the counters and walls. It makes the booths look old and tired…so depressing. Let's get out of here. Where's the blueberry cordial?"

I stepped over papers and pots. My foot crunched on shattered plates as I made my way to the cabinet where I hoped my blueberry cordial was waiting. On the bottom shelf: four pint jars filled with the beautiful blue liquid sat untouched and waiting for me to rescue them.

"I may as well take them all," I said and carefully packed them in a small basket lying on the floor. "No point in tempting fate after they survived one disaster."

With my basket secured at my side, we tiptoed over the debris back toward the door. Now that I had my treasure, I couldn't get out fast enough.

A violent banging on the door made my blood drain to my toes.

"What should we do, Dani?" Lily whispered.

I put my finger to my lips, hoping that if we were quiet, the person would leave.

Pip, unfortunately, didn't understand my strategy and she charged the door as ferocious as a mama bear protecting her cubs, barking to let the intruder know she meant business.

"Lily? Are you in there with Dani? Open the door. I need to talk to you." Rhonda's angry voice competed with her pounding and Pip's ruckus.

I yanked the door open, hoping to catch her by surprise and reverse any advantage she thought she might have over us. When her knuckles hit air, she tipped forward, almost into my arms but caught herself on the doorframe.

"Oh, hello, Rhonda. So nice to see you," I smiled deciding the best strategy was to kill her with kindness. I waited for Lily and Pip to slip past us before I pulled the door closed, effectively blocking the interior from Rhonda's snooping eyes.

Rhonda grabbed Lily's hand. "I want to apologize to you. I think I took my frustration with Ray out on you, but maybe we could work on building a positive relationship?"

"Now that I'm your boss?" Lily said. I swallowed a laugh as she got straight to the heart of the matter.

"Sure, that's part of it but I think I can help you with the business. I *want* to help you." Rhonda tucked her hair behind her ears, and I was almost blinded by two brilliant sparkles.

"Your ear is better?" I asked. Did I have to cross her off the suspect list now?

Rhonda touched her ear and twirled the diamond star that had been missing the last time I saw her. "Yes. Finally. So, Lily, what do you say?"

"I have a lot of questions, but I don't see any reason why we can't work on smoothing out our differences. First things first, though. I'm planning a reception at Rose's house after Ray's funeral, so, let your parents know, okay?"

"Certainly. They'll appreciate that, Lily."

I tugged on Lily's arm. "I'm taking Lily over to

talk to Frank and Nick about last minute details. Gotta go!"

Lily climbed into the MG and made room for Pip, who didn't seem to mind in the least. "Why do I have to go with you and not take my own car?" she said when I jumped in the driver's seat and turned the key.

"It's all I could think of to get away from Rhonda. You aren't forgiving her just like that, are you?"

Lily jutted her chin out and stared straight ahead.

"You are. I can tell. Just don't say I didn't warn you, Lil. Once a snake, always a snake."

"I think you're wrong this time. She was always competing with Ray and now she doesn't have to. I believe people *can* change."

Lily couldn't help it. She always saw the best in people even if there was no best. "Right, like Ray changed?" I mumbled that comment but I'm positive she heard me. I hoped I was wrong about Rhonda for Lily's sake, but I wasn't going to bet on this one.

I turned into the funeral home parking lot, and for the sake of a better spot, I pulled in behind the hearse. Hopefully it didn't have to pick up a body anytime soon.

With no more than one foot inside the door, Frank spotted us and gestured for us to follow him to his office. He mostly ignored me but hovered over Lily. "Nice to see you, have a seat. How are you doing, Lily?"

"As well as can be expected," she said with a little flutter of her eyelashes.

Safe answer with so many hidden meanings. "Frank. You found your earring," I said when he rubbed the glittery star.

He smiled. "Actually." He leaned toward us and lowered his voice. "I was lucky to get my hands on the last pair at Creative Designs but *please* don't tell Rhonda. She was furious when she found out I lost it. Somehow, I misplaced the one I was wearing *and* its mate. Kind of embarrassing since I'm not usually so careless." He shrugged. "I guess I've been too distracted with everything that was going on."

"Oh, I know what you mean," I said. "The fake funeral, buying this building, and then Ray murdered ... so much all at once."

"You know about the building?" he asked with genuine confusion on his face. "Ray didn't want anyone to know until after the closing. As a matter of fact, the closing was supposed to be after the fake funeral. Right, Lily?"

I looked at my best friend and couldn't help but have a sinking feeling in my gut that she'd kept yet another secret from me. "You knew all along, Lil?"

With her eyes drilling a hole into Frank, she said to me, "Frank's lying. I didn't know *anything* about a closing. I told you I didn't sign that sales agreement." Lily's voice was cold, hard, and angry.

"You didn't sign it?" Frank asked. I couldn't tell if his surprised look was genuine or good acting. "Ray said you finally agreed to sell to us when we agreed to have the fake funeral. He said it was all your idea to have that silly affair to kick off your reconciliation. Then, you stormed out. I have to say, you made a lot of people unhappy when you didn't follow the plan."

Lily stood up and stomped right over to Frank and stuck her finger in his face. "You have it all wrong. *Ray* planned that funeral. *Ray* forged my signature. And *Ray*...I don't know." Her hands flew in the air in a gesture of frustration.

"Got himself killed?" I filled in for her.

"This certainly is a giant tangled web of deception." Frank stood up and backed away from Lily. "What are we going to do?" His hands trembled a little before he steadied them on the back of a chair. "How about I get us all a drink and we can try to relax and sort this out? There's some delicious blueberry cordial in Nick's office. It adds a nice kick when added to carbonated water. I'll ask him to bring it in."

"No…no thanks, Frank. I just remembered that Lily has an appointment with…the florist. I've got to get her over there right now." I picked up Pip, grabbed Lily's arm, and backed out of his office.

"What's going on, Dani?" Lily whispered as I dragged her down the hall and outside.

"Get in the car," I ordered.

Once we were locked inside, I called the police department and asked for Detective Crenshaw. Lily stared at me like I had three heads, but she didn't say anything.

It felt like hours before I heard a voice. "Speaking."

"It's Dani. Meet me at the funeral home."

"What? Why are you whispering?"

"Just meet me here at the funeral home, AJ, and hurry!" I hung up but clung to the phone like it might be a lifeline. If AJ didn't arrive shortly, it probably would be.

"Dani?" Lily implored. "What is going on? Did

Ray's ghost return and tell you who murdered him? Or are you falling apart because of the stress?"

Lily was trying to make a joke, but her forehead was etched with worry lines.

"I know who killed Ray, Lil. I know who did it."

CHAPTER TWENTY-SIX

I drummed my fingers on the steering wheel. "Come on AJ. Hurry up," I muttered.

Nick walked out the side door toward the hearse and saw he was blocked. He walked toward my window with murder in his eyes. Pip jumped from Lily's lap to mine, scratched at the window and barked ferociously. "Good girl, Pip."

Nick banged on the window. "Move your car. I have to leave."

I shrugged and held my hands out. "Sorry, Nick. It won't start. I left the lights on and the battery's dead." I felt Lily staring at me. At this point, she had to be beyond confused.

Nick paced in front of my car.

I kept looking in my rear-view mirror

wondering if Nick would jump in a different vehicle and take off.

At last, AJ's car pulled in behind the MG. I got out, looked at Nick, smiled, and signaled him to give me a minute before I met AJ. He slid out of his SUV and I quickly said, "I need a jump."

I think I saw steam come out of his ears. "I'm not a road service person, Dani." He stomped to the back to his car, I guess to get his jumper cables, with me on his tail.

I glanced over my shoulder, relieved that Nick was occupied on his phone. "Nick is the killer," I whispered.

AJ stiffened and whispered back. "What? Are you sure?"

"Absolutely. He *stole* a bottle of blueberry cordial from the diner, AJ. I had five bottles left before Ray was murdered and today there were only four. Frank said Nick had a bottle in his office. And, he had a blue stain on the cuff of his shirt. The only way Nick could have a bottle of my cordial is if he *stole* it after *he* killed Ray. Plus, he knew Frank lost an earring. I think he planted it at the diner after he killed Ray." I had to pause and take a breath after all that.

"Your battery isn't dead?"

"No, of course it isn't! I was trying to keep Nick here until you arrived."

"Good thinking, Dani." He smiled and patted my shoulder before he approached Nick.

I sagged against his car. Lily got out of the MG, and Pip leaped through the open door. She charged right at Nick, clamped onto his pant leg and growled and pulled with all her ten pounds of fury.

"Get your dog off me, Dani. What's wrong with her?" Nick screeched.

I rushed over and tried to wrestle Pip away from Nick. She twisted and threw her head from side to side, tugging like a maniac on Nick's pant leg, never letting go until it ripped, sending me backwards. But I managed to hang on to Pip.

"My pants!" Nick yelled, full of outrage.

"Your leg." I pointed as I stared at the last bit of evidence that AJ would need to arrest Nick.

"She bit me," he screamed.

AJ bent down. "There's no blood. That didn't just happen."

"You're right about that, AJ, because Pip didn't bite him today. Right, Nick? She bit him when she was trying to defend Ray, when *you* killed him, when *you* planted Frank's earring in the diner, and when *you* stole my blueberry cordial." I blurted out all the pieces of this mixed up murder. "Why?"

Bits of spittle formed at the edge of Nick's mouth. His eyes blazed with rage. I could see excuses trying to push through the frustration on his face, but finally he blurted out in a stream of anger, "They were trying to push me out of the business," his words full of defensiveness as though that would justify murder.

"Frank and Rhonda had it all figured out. They tried to keep everything secret from me, but I heard their whispers when they thought they were alone. Frank had that deal to buy the building all wrapped up. Where would that leave *me?*"

He covered his face with his hands, and it sounded like he was sobbing, but if he was going after pity from me, he missed by a mile.

"Yes, I followed Ray," he admitted. "But only to talk him out of that sale. He laughed at me and tried to push me away. I really don't know what happened, but something snapped inside." Still on the ground, he looked up at AJ. "I had to defend myself." He exhaled and his whole body seemed to shrink as if he just realized he'd confessed to murder. "Frank's earring must have fallen out of my pocket when I struggled with Ray."

"Why did you take the blueberry cordial?" A silly question, but I had to know.

He shrugged and fiddled with his cuff with the incriminating blue stain. "The cabinet door was open and with the mess all around, those jars of blue caught my eye. It was just an impulse. Who would miss it?"

Who indeed? And who was I to think I'd ever be able to understand someone else's motives.

I hugged Pip until she yelped, but I didn't dare let her loose. Instead, I put her back in the MG, while AJ got Nick in the back of his SUV. Before he left, he walked over to me. "I'll need all the information from you again. You put it all together because of the blueberry cordial, huh? That must be some powerful stuff. I'd love a sample."

"Come to Sea Breeze after Ray's funeral. We'll be toasting his final send off with my blueberry cordial. I think that's fitting, don't you?"

AJ laughed. "You're something else, Danielle Mackenzie."

Hadn't I heard that before?

T he Little Dog Diner had to close indefinitely
    while Rose planned the renovations, I made
the most of my unexpected free time enjoying her
patio. We had discussed the positives and negatives
of my moving in with her and mutually agreed that
Sea Breeze would be my home, at least until the
diner was renovated and open for business again. If
things worked out? Maybe longer. Pip didn't
complain as long as I took her for walks on the
beach every day so she could chase the seagulls and
snap at the waves to her heart's content.

Ava and Marty had returned to their luxury
apartment in New York City, so I didn't have to
worry about Pip attacking the crazy yoga-lady
during our beach meanderings.

I contemplated the past several weeks while I sat
on the patio, as a warm gentle breeze ruffled my
curls and a colony of gulls rested on one leg at the
water's edge.

One problem had sorted itself out while I
procrastinated. Lily decided to remain at the Little
Dog Diner. She and Rhonda came to an agreement
with the real estate business after Lily realized it
wasn't her cup of tea.

My head fell against the back of the chair and I
closed my eyes. The sun warmed my face as I

drifted off into a place where crashing waves and squawking birds filled me with nature's special brand of music.

"Can I join you?"

My eyes popped open. Blinded by the bright sunshine, I lifted my hand to shade my eyes. "Luke? You're back?"

"I'm back, Dani. Back in Misty Harbor for good this time." He had a few more wrinkles than I remembered from a few short weeks ago. I would let him talk about all he'd been through when he was ready. For now, I hoped he could relax and enjoy the view with me.

I patted the chair next to me knowing I had a big foolish grin from one ear to the other. "Sit down. We'll share a refreshing drink to toast your return." Filling two glasses from the pitcher on the small round table between us, I handed Luke a glass of half blueberry cordial and half lemonade and tapped my glass against his. "Welcome back."

He took a sip. "This is delicious." He sipped more. "It goes down too easily. What *is* this blend of bubbly blue beverage?"

I laughed. "It's my blueberry cordial made with berries from *your* farm mixed with lemonade. Very easy to make and easier to drink. I'm sure you could sell it at your farm stand faster than I could make it. Or," I smiled shyly, "in your bed and breakfast if you go that route."

"I'll need to sample a few more glasses before committing to that project." He held his glass out for seconds. I think his grin matched mine. I'd take that as a sign he was beginning to heal from his loss.

Sitting here looking at Blueberry Bay, and knowing I'd never find a more beautiful spot anywhere made my heart sing with happiness. This was an essential constant in my life that I couldn't live without.

"Thanks for stopping by, Luke."

"Thanks for being my friend, Dani."

"No problem."

I was beyond thrilled to have Luke back in my life.

WHAT'S NEXT?

As it turns out quilting is the deadly new fad people are just dying to try… And here I thought the annual quilt auction would be a boring way to spend an evening!

One big murder in my tiny hometown was more than I ever wanted to see, but now the death toll has risen to two. Eek!

Hey, at least I've got my favorite ten-pound bundle of mischief at my side for good. My Jack Russell buddy, Pip, and I are experienced amateur detectives now and we're more than ready to put another tough case to bed.

The problem is that the murder victim had no known enemies, which begs the question: Who would actually want her dead? For this tricky catering gig, it looks like we'll be serving up suspects instead of dessert. Can we catch the killer in time to save the fundraiser… and maybe even some lives along the way?

Get your copy here!
https://sweetpromisepress.com/Serving

SNEAK PEEK: SERVING UP SUSPECTS

The Little Dog Diner sparkled in the early morning sun when I parked my MG in front.

It wasn't only the bright white siding and red trim on the outside that made it stand out. Rose Mackenzie, my grandma, had remodeled the inside with new chrome stools at the shiny counter, and red booths along the side. She had spared no expense when she hired Luke Sinclair—blueberry farmer wrapped in carpenter gear and, yes, I had a soft spot for him.

Luke pulled off the transformation flawlessly. He had a touch for making everything tasteful and charming. Judging by the stream of customers, the locals and tourists of Misty Harbor, Maine, agreed.

When I hurried inside the door to start my shift, I quickly glanced in the decorative oval mirror, Luke's last handcrafted touch.

A stranger caught my attention in the reflection. This early in the morning usually brought in the regulars, so this guy stood out like a shark out of water.

"Dani!" Lily Lemay, my best friend since forever, called from behind the counter. "A little help over here? Please?"

At the sound of my name, I took one last fleeting glance at the stranger's dark, eerily penetrating image in the mirror. He caught me looking at him, and the corners of his mouth turned up, sending shivers tingling along my spine. Definitely not in a good way.

With a quick fluff of my out of control auburn curls, as if that was why I had looked in the mirror to begin with, I stiffened my shoulders, grabbed a blue apron covered with bright red images of lobsters, and joined Lily behind the counter.

I sidled up to her and whispered so only she could hear, "Who *is* that guy?"

"I have no idea, but I wish he'd leave," she said, the stress of serving the early morning rush evident in the sharp tone she sent his way. "He's been sitting there ever since I put up the Open sign, sipping on that same cup of black coffee the whole time." She flicked her long blonde braid over her shoulder and glanced at the stranger.

"He smiled at me," I said, sorting the pastries in the glass-fronted case beneath the register.

"Okay. Creepy." Lily's lips turned down in distaste.

The diner door opened, ringing the overhead bell and announcing the arrival of new customers.

"Thank goodness," Lily said, pulling on thick, quilted mitts, "more regulars. He'll get lost in the crowd." She opened the oven and pulled out a tray of brownies.

I inhaled deeply, savoring the rich chocolate aroma and waved my hand to direct more of the delicious scent my way. With one deep breath, I could have vacuumed the whole, delicious batch right into my mouth. "Chocolate. Sweet creamy chocolate. Want me to cut them?" I grabbed a long slicing knife.

"Ha! I don't think so," Lily replied. "First, they need to cool, and second, with that drool at the edge of your mouth, I'm afraid every single one will end up in your stomach. Anyway, these are a special order. Remember?"

I dabbed at my mouth before realizing that Lily was exaggerating about any drool. "A special order?" I knew we prepared dozens of desserts for the quilt auction, but brownies weren't on the list.

"Sue Ellen is going crazy with preparations for her quilt auction tonight. On top of her original dessert request, she insisted we add something extra chocolaty to satisfy the biggest chocoholic." Lily shrugged. "I think she meant herself. Our brownies are already rich, but she wants chocolate frosting slathered on top. I suspect there could be a few sugar overdoses." She leaned closer to me as though some of the customers might hear. "Person-ally, the chocolate frosting is over the top sweet for *me*, but what Sue Ellen wants, Sue Ellen gets. Right?"

"Oh, yeah, she certainly has that I-don't-take-no for an answer personality." My eyes were glued to the brownies. Too sweet? No way.

Lily elbowed me out of my brownie fixation and nodded toward the pastry case. "Your creepy admirer is eyeing the pastries. You'd better get over there and help him. I'll handle the breakfast orders."

"I hate starting the day with a customer that unappealing," I mumbled so only Lily could hear but she had already moved to a family of five at a nearby table and was taking their order.

I welcomed the barrier of the pastry case as I forced up a smile for the stranger. "Does anything appeal to you this morning?" I said as brightly as I could. What was it about him that sent shivers down my neck?

"As a matter of fact, just about everything in here is making my taste buds rev into overdrive but," he looked up into my eyes, "I'm looking for Rose Mackenzie. She's supposed to meet me here."

With my face as neutral as I could manage, I asked, "And you are?" There was nothing about this man that made me connect him with my grandma.

"Rudy."

"Oh," I said, probably sounding like a doofus. The name sparked my memory but, like so often happens, the image I had was a far cry from this man standing in front of me. For some reason, I expected a tall, dark, and handsome man, but this guy was the complete opposite.

"Rudy Genova, the videographer?" I made sure to say it loud enough so Lily would hear and put an end to wondering about whether this mystery man was a mass murderer or a harmless customer. "That's why you were staring at me earlier?"

"Yeah. You look like Rose. Are you sisters?" His lips turned up at the edges. I guessed it was supposed to be a smile.

That was quite the come-on. Not that I didn't like being compared to my elegant grandmother, but, come on, there was fifty years separating us. "She's my grandmother, but people always confuse us as sisters." I wondered if he caught my sarcasm.

He leaned over the top of the pastry display. I leaned away, not sure if he was planning to climb over the barrier. "Now that I'm closer, I can see how much younger you are, and you beat Rose in the looks department, hands down." He wiggled his eyebrows. "Don't tell her I said that, though, okay?"

I shifted uncomfortably from one foot to the other. I asked, in an attempt to move the conversation away from this awkwardness, "Rose said she'd meet you here?"

Now that I remembered who this mystery man was, the guy Rose had told me was helping with her website, I gave Rudy a more thorough inspection— from his shiny black hair, coal dark eyes, and stocky build, which put him a few inches taller than my five-foot-five height, to his black jeans and black leather boots that looked out of place for a summer day in our Maine seaside town. Where *was* Rose to save me from this man?

"That's what she said, the Little Dog Diner. You know, it's a quaint little place." He swiveled his head around like a bobblehead doll and asked, "We gonna do any of the filming for her website here?"

Before I could catch my breath and figure out the proper answer to this question, a voice, with a slight southern twang, boomed through the diner. I turned to see two women.

Sue Ellen wagged her finger and moaned, "Rudy. Rudy. Rudy. Bless your heart. You arrived and never let me know you're here?" Her eyes narrowed as she delivered a fake, "Naughty, naughty," scold at her friend.

I sighed with relief and had to admit to myself that I had never been so happy to see Sue Ellen Baer walk into the diner. With her voluminous red dress ballooning around her, she moved toward her prey like a bullfighter wielding a cape. It wasn't just her oversized personality that filled up the café. Her extra-large leather tote bag banged into the side of her leg with each step and with the top gaping open, it was ready for every single brownie to jump inside. I chuckled at that image.

Sue Ellen was one of those curvy women who

always looked stylish, though having an unlimited budget for the latest fashions and frequent trips to the hair and nail salons didn't hurt, either. She managed quite nicely on her inheritance from her late father which allowed her to indulge in all of life's pleasures plus build one of the biggest houses in Misty Harbor.

"Sue Ellen?" Rudy extended both arms, wrapping her in a big bear hug. Then he backed up, letting his gaze run from Sue Ellen's bleached blonde curly hair to her five-inch heels. "You are a sight for sore eyes in that ruby red dress."

"Oh, Rudy." Sue Ellen giggled and covered her mouth. A pink splotch grew on both cheeks. "I bet you say that to all the girls."

Girls? I thought. Sue Ellen was at least thirty years beyond her *girl* days.

Rudy winked at me before he continued his flattery. "Nonsense, Sue Ellen. You can't be a day older than—"

"Shush!" Sue Ellen put her finger across Rudy's lips. "Stop right now and don't embarrass me, Rudy." She pulled another woman closer. "You haven't met Judith Manning yet. My indispensable last-minute detail-fixer for the auction. You know me, I see the big picture."

Judith lingered behind Sue Ellen, content to be out of the spotlight.

Meanwhile, Sue Ellen's arms swirled in an arc above her head. "Judith figures out how to turn my vision into a reality worthy of this monumental occasion."

Judith smiled, but I could tell her heart wasn't in it. She had the look of someone who spent most of her time on the outside looking in rather than smack in the center where Sue Ellen flourished. Her dark skirt and white blouse, along with practical black pumps made a stark contrast to Sue Ellen's flamboyant style.

She held her hand out. "Nice to meet you, Rudy. Sue Ellen has built you up into someone capable of performing filming magic. I hope you can live up to this pedestal she has you on."

"Oh, don't mind her, Rudy. Judith, unlike me, sees problems around every corner." From what I'd heard, Judith had a few problems of her own, but maybe that was gossip. "Come over to one of the booths and have coffee with us." Sue Ellen continued. "I've got a few last-minute details I want to discuss for your filming tonight at the quilt auction." She lowered her voice, for the first time since she'd entered the diner, "Dani, sweetheart, could you bring over three of those spectacular looking fruit thingies?"

"Sue Ellen, I haven't learned to read minds yet." I smiled and bit the inside of my cheek as a reminder to be patient. "Is it this cream cheese square with raspberries on Lily's flakey pastry or this blueberry tart glazed with apricot jam?"

Sue Ellen bobbed her body back and forth, considering the offerings, and swinging that ruby red fabric a foot to each side of her legs. "Too many delicious choices. Just put two of each on a plate, that way, I won't be second-guessing myself. By the way, are all the desserts ready for the auction tonight?"

"Just finishing up the last of the chocolate covered brownies that you added last night, Sue Ellen," Lily said with a wink at me. "I had a devil of a time keeping them away from our own chocoholic."

"Oh, I know." Sue Ellen closed her eyes and shivered with passion. "Chocolate is impossible to resist. Could you put a few in a bag for me to take this morning?"

"No problem," Lily said.

Rose, sunglasses perched on the top of her head

and her straw hat tucked under her arm, glided into the diner; a woman on a mission. "Oh, Rudy, I'm sorry I'm late. Sometimes, I can't get out of my own way. Let me grab some blueberry whoopie pies to go and you can follow me to Blueberry Acres. I want to show you one of Misty Harbor's oldest businesses while I explain my vision for my website."

Rudy turned away from Sue Ellen and stared at Rose, showing hesitation about which woman to follow.

I was a step ahead of Rose, packing blueberry whoopie pies in a box for her as soon as I heard her destination. "Packed and ready to go. I put in plenty for Luke and his dad since I know these are their favorite, especially with their blueberries in the recipe."

"I could kiss you, Dani." Rose tucked the box under her arm. "Okay, then. It's looking busy here this morning, so we'll get out of your way.

I hoped that Rose's enthusiasm carried her through this latest project. She wanted this film on her website for the Blueberry Bay Grapevine, her weekly paper for all things of interest in the Blueberry Bay area.

"Don't forget, you volunteered Lily and me for

dessert delivery and setup at Sue Ellen's house for the auction."

"Oh, right. I'll keep Rudy busy for the morning and then Sue Ellen gets him for the afternoon. I'll see you back at Sea Breeze tonight, Dani. And, don't worry about Pip while you're working. I'll take her with me."

I looked out the window at my terrier. Pip sat quietly in front of her water dish like a famous movie star, enjoying the morning sunshine and the many pats from residents walking by who'd become her friends since I'd rescued her from a horrible fate. Rose had her adorned with a hot pink bandana that complimented Pip's white hair and brown ears. By her upturned face and wagging tail, I suspected she knew exactly how cute she looked, too.

Rose took Rudy's arm with one hand and balancing the box of whoopie pies with the other, she left exactly how she'd arrived—like a seagull soaring over Blueberry Bay, ready for anything.

Get your copy here!

https://sweetpromisepress.com/Serving

WHAT'S AFTER THAT?

I always thought weddings were supposed to be about joining lives… Not ending them.

But when an unexpected guest shows up dead on the beach and the groom seems to be hiding more than just cold feet, I need to take my chef's hat off and don my deerstalker once again.

Who was this mysterious stranger that came to town claiming to be a long lost relative, and why is she now dead? Who is the groom really, and are his intentions for my friend pure?

Deceit—like revenge—may be a dish best served cold, but I'm not quite sure any of us have the stomach for it. Wedding bells are ringing, but might they also be the death knell? And is the killer really going to be satisfied with just one victim when two could be twice as nice?

Oh, dear. Pip and I certainly have our work cut out for us this time…

Get your copy here!
https://sweetpromisepress.com/Dishing

MORE BLUEBERRY BAY

Welcome to Blueberry Bay, a scenic region of Maine peppered with quaint small towns and home to a shocking number of mysteries. If you loved this book, then make sure to check out its sister series from other talented Cozy Mystery authors...

Pet Whisperer P.I.
By Molly Fitz

Glendale is home to Blueberry Bay's first ever talking cat detective. Along with his ragtag gang of human and animal helpers, Octo-Cat is determined to save the day... so long as it doesn't interfere with his schedule. Start with book one, *Kitty Confidential*, which is now available to buy or borrow! Visit www.MollyMysteries.com for more.

Little Dog Diner
By Emmie Lyn

Misty Cove boasts the best lobster rolls in all of Blueberry Bay. There's another thing that's always on the menu, too. Murder! Dani and her little terrier, Pip, have a knack for being in the wrong place at the wrong time... which often lands them smack in the middle of a fresh, new murder mystery and in the crosshairs of one cunning criminal after the next. Start with book one, *Mixing Up Murder*, which is now available to buy or borrow! Visit www.EmmieLynBooks.com for more.

Shelf Indulgence
By S.E. Babin

Dewdrop Springs is home to Tattered Pages, a popular bookshop with an internet cafe, a grumpy Persian cat named Poppy, and some of the most suspicious characters you'll ever meet. And poor Dakota Adair has just inherited it all. She'll need to

make peace with her new cat and use all her book
smarts to catch a killer or she might be the next to
wind up dead in the stacks. Book one, *Hardback
Homicide*, will be coming soon. Keep an eye
on www.QuirkyCozy.com for more.

Haunted Housekeeping
By R.A. Muth

Cooper's Cove is home to Blueberry Bay's premier
estate cleaning service. Tori and Hazel, the ill-fated
proprietors of Bubbles and Troubles, are prepared
to uncover a few skeletons. But when a real one
turns up, they'll have to solve the mystery quickly if
they're going to save their reputations--and their
lives. Book one, *The Squeaky Clean Skeleton*, will be
coming soon. Keep an eye
on www.QuirkyCozy.com for more.

The Kindergarten Coven
By F.M. Storm

Quiet, secluded, and most importantly, far away
from his annoying magical family, Guy couldn't
wait to start a new life on Caraway Island.

Unfortunately, he hadn't counted on his four-year-old daughter coming into her own witchy powers early… or on her accidentally murdering one of the PTO moms. Oops! Book one, *Stay-at-Home Sorcery*, will be coming soon. Keep an eye on www.QuirkyCozy.com for more.

I hope you enjoyed this book.

Click here to sign up for my newsletter and never miss a new release.

ABOUT EMMIE LYN

Emmie Lyn shares her world with her husband, a rescue terrier named Underdog, and a black cat named Ziggy. When she's not busy thinking of ways to kill off a character, she loves enjoying tea and chocolate in her flower garden, hiking, or spending time near the ocean. Find out more at Emmielynbooks.com.

MORE FROM EMMIE

COZY MYSTERIES

Little Dog Diner

Mixing Up Murder

COMING SOON

Serving Up Suspects

Dishing Up Deceit

Cooking Up Chaos

Catering Up Catastrophe

🍴

ROMANTIC SUSPENSE

Gold Coast Retrievers

Helping Hanna

Shielding Shelly